THE
ANNOTATED
HUNTING
OF THE SNARK

THE DEFINITIVE EDITION

LEWIS CARROLL,
as sketched by Harry Furness, illustrator of
Carroll's novel *Sylvie and Bruno*.

W. W. NORTON & COMPANY
New York · London

THE ANNOTATED HUNTING OF THE SNARK

THE DEFINITIVE EDITION

The full text of

Lewis Carroll's

great nonsense epic

The Hunting of the Snark

ORIGINAL ILLUSTRATIONS BY

HENRY HOLIDAY

EDITED WITH A PREFACE AND NOTES BY

MARTIN GARDNER

INTRODUCTION BY

ADAM GOPNIK

For information about permission to reproduce selections from this book, write to
Permissions, W. W. Norton & Company, Inc., 500 Fifth Avenue, New York, NY 10110

Manufacturing by Courier Westford
Book design by Joanne Metsch
Production manager: Julia Druskin

Library of Congress Cataloging-in-Publication Data

The annotated Hunting of the snark : the full text of Lewis Carroll's great nonsense epic
The hunting of the snark / original illustrations by Henry Holiday ; edited with a preface and notes
by Martin Gardner ; introduction by Adam Gopnik.—Definitive ed.
p. cm.
Includes bibliographical references.
ISBN-13: 978-0-393-06242-7 (hardcover)
ISBN-10: 0-393-06242-2 (hardcover)
1. Carroll, Lewis, 1832–1898 Hunting of the snark. 2. Nonsense verses, English—
History and criticism. I. Carroll, Lewis, 1832–1898.
Hunting of the snark. II. Gardner, Martin, 1914–
PR4611.H83A85 2006
821'.8—dc22
2006018928

W. W. Norton & Company, Inc., 500 Fifth Avenue, New York, N.Y. 10110
www.wwnorton.com

W. W. Norton & Company Ltd., Castle House, 75/76 Wells Street, London W1T 3QT

1 2 3 4 5 6 7 8 9 0

With love to

RACHEL OTT

But, should the play
Prove piercing earnest,
Should the glee glaze
In Death's stiff stare,

Would not the fun
Look too expensive!
Would not the jest
Have crawled too far!

EMILY DICKINSON

CONTENTS

ILLUSTRATIONS

INTRODUCTION TO
THE ANNOTATED HUNTING
OF THE SNARK

BY ADAM GOPNIK

A FRABJOUS day dawns, and a large callooh and heartfelt callay are shouted out at this reappearance of Martin Gardner's *The Annotated Hunting of the Snark*. First published in 1961, it was the second of the ambitious (and, in their day, still quite novel) annotations of Lewis Carroll's major works that Gardner, the extraordinary American "philosophical scrivener," accomplished in the 1960s.

It was a necessary piece of work, for, more so than the Alice books, whose annotated edition preceded this one, *The Hunting Of The Snark* demands explication. Lewis Carroll's second most important masterwork—after only the Alice books in quality, and before *Sylvie & Bruno* and *Sylvie & Bruno Concluded* in importance—the *Snark* was first published in 1876, a decade after the Alice books had made their extraordinary splash in Victorian England, a splash whose after-spill, lapping over into everything from animated film to surrealist poetry, continues to this day. Written by Carroll (the pen name, of course, of the Oxford mathematician, clergyman, and logician Charles Dodgson) as, appropriately enough, a gift to his second-best child friend, Gertrude Chataway, the Snark is "Jabberwocky" writ large—a "nonsense" poem expanded to epic length, in eight "fits," as Carroll calls his stanzas.

It tells, like the famous shorter poem, the tale of a bizarre but on its own terms sensible quest: a boatful of searchers, under the captainship of a Bellman, attempt to find a mythical and valuable creature called the Snark. One of their number, however, the "hero," a Baker (all of the searchers have names that begin with a *B*, from a Beaver to a Butcher) has secret and dreadful knowledge; the Snark, when found, *may* turn out to be another kind of creature, the awful

Boojum. If it is, the Baker knows that he will "softly and suddenly vanish away / and never be met with again!" The search of the crew for its Snark, under the pressure of both their hope and the Baker's dread, is the matter of the poem.

And a wonderful comic-epic poem the *Snark* remains, filled with writing as wild and funny as anything Carroll, or anyone else, has achieved. Its best inventions—the perfectly blank map which the Bellman uses to search for the Snark, the long list of "unmistakable marks" of the Snark—have that distinctive Carrollian quality of being at once utterly absurd and universally applicable. But the *Snark* is also, and has been recognized as such since its first publication, a *dark* poem, a poem which, with its agonized hero, touches themes of existential and even sexual fright that are, for Carroll, remarkably open, impossible to ignore or put down to overambitious readings. This makes *The Annotated Hunting of the Snark*, perhaps even more than Gardner's great *Annotated Alice*, vital to a new generation of readers: the long, strange, and in many ways sinister poem has never felt more peculiarly apropos. We live our lives in America, now, in fits that involve many Snarks, possible Boojums.

Even more than the Alice books, *Snark* is a masterpiece that benefits from being opened up. Not explicated, or deconstructed, or explained—simply *read*, and by a first-rate mind, with those readings placed in the margins of the text. That is what Gardner's annotated texts supply, and it is the inspiration that he has given to subsequent generations of similar editions. Gardner's ambitions in the annotations of Carroll are not pedantic—there is little worrying detail about dates or editions—but they are, I think, interpretive, and Gardner's reading of the comic poem has been, for this reader at least, inseparable from a forty-year love for it. What we get here is an extraordinarily smart reading of the poem from the point of view of a reader who cares deeply and knows a lot about its logical, philosophical, and—no other word comes to mind—its existential matter. Gardner's annotations don't attempt to show us what the book "really" meant to its original readers, much less what it really means now—they show instead, and, winningly, all that it *can* mean to one remarkably attentive reader. Like light, the poem's spectrum of ideas bends and separates as it passes through the prism of a loving reader's mind. Gardener's annotated text rests on the truth that a poem knows itself better than we can know it, but that we know our own minds better after we've read it than we did before.

The Alice books are classics of wit, and remain either as lucid as you like or as deep as you choose to dive. But the *Snark* is a surrealist text properly so called, a work, like a Max Ernst collage—those wonderful assemblies of advertising imagery and dream imagery weirdly juxtaposed—whose local details all make sense and whose global meaning makes none, or at least none in the literal and obvious sense. It works hard at a surface plausibility and then leaves us bewildered about just what has happened, or is happening. Everything in the *Snark* seems to be laid out with the neat table-setting order of an allegorical poem: the ship goes to sea with its blank map and its crew; we learn, at the proper epic moment, of the five unmistakable signs of the Snark, from its peculiar taste to its unaccountable fondness for bathing-machines, those bizarre mobile dressing rooms that enabled the modest Victorian to change into a bathing costume at the very edge of the ocean, away from prying eyes (the Snark we learn, takes this fondness to the edge of madness: "Which it constantly carries about, / And believes that they add to the beauty of scenes– / A sentiment open to doubt") and think, at first, that it must mean . . . something.

Yet the more we read, the more we feel that the poem is genuinely dreamlike in the sense of being lucid in its incidents and disturbingly illogical in its acts. Everything happens in sequence—we learn of the Bellman's rule-of-three ("What I tell you three times is true"), we are instructed in the Baker's dread, we begin the quest, all in order and as we should—but nothing that happens makes sense. The only certainty we have lies in that ominous warning whose exact meaning is the most uncertain thing in the poem—" 'But oh, beamish nephew, beware of the day, / If your Snark be a Boojum! For then / You will softly and silently vanish away, / And never be heard of again!' "

No poem could seem, in its suggestive depths and half-lit wonders, more neatly allegorical, and, from its first appearance, critics have sought to find an allegory in it. Is the Snark perhaps a symbol of the Absolute loved by German idealist philosophers, as the American philosopher F. C. S. Schiller suggested in a famous reading? Or a symbol of worldly riches? Or of God? And is the fatal Boojum, its evil twin, a companion symbol of what we find at the end of our search for the ultimate and transcendent thing, God or riches or the Absolute? The poem defeats any of these attempts to restrict it to a single reading, even as its potential applicability is ever expanding. We all go out on our quests with a blank map; we all fear that our Snark, whatever it may be, will turn out to be a Boojum.

Yet surrealist works (and if the *Snark* is not the first surrealist poem, it is hard to say what is), though meant to defy logic, invite and welcome a certain kind of minute scholarship. It is helpful to know, in registering the passage of the banal into the baleful, which is exactly which. Gardner's annotated books have, in this way, something in common with Nabokov's lectures on the literature of fantasy, with their relentless stress on the *it-ness* of literature—on the kind of bug Gregor became or the shape of Gogol's lost nose. Gardner does something similar: he lets us enter a dreamworld through its connection to the fact world. By entering into a weird book as an empirical document, as something that reports on the world, it allows us to isolate and better understand the act of imagination peculiar to the poet. We know what's seen and known from what's made and felt.

Gardner accomplishes this in part by restoring to the poem's side some of the ideas and contexts that would have been self-evident to its original readers. The then-famous Victorian case of the Tichborne claimant, for instance, in which an illiterate butcher from Australia claimed to be the long-lost son of a British aristocrat, was thought at the time to have influenced the poem. Gardner rightly thinks it fairly remote from Carroll's intention, but the invocation and explanation of the case at least reminds us of the absurdity of the Victorian wig-and-pomposity trials that Carroll loved to mock, and whose unintended public nonsense is part of the background of the willed private nonsense of the poem. Or, at a simpler level, we learn what a billiard-marker actually is. (And Gardner adds the nice reflection that a billiard-marker actually has a cameo in one of the Sherlock Holmes stories as well; he walks past the Diogenes Club window where Sherlock watches the street with his brother Mycroft in "The Greek Interpreter"—a nice, Borgesian invocation of an imaginary world, encompassing both Carroll's and Doyle's inventions, as complex as this "real" one.)

At the same time Gardner is a reader who seeks not to make sense of Carroll's writing but to make clearer nonsense of it: he wants us to understand why Carroll's comedy anticipates scientific ideas and philosophical problems that his time could scarcely have imagined. We learn, for instance, that the Bellman's rule-of-three plays its role in what was, in 1961, the newborn science of cybernetics.

Gardner always rejects the idea that Carroll was engaged in writing texts encrypted with hidden significance, as in the more recent attempts to "read" *Alice* as an allegory of British politics, or as an allegory of anything. He is especially, and rightly, hard on psychoanalytic interpretations of the text (though even a resolute non-Freudian can see something in those bathing-machines). But he does believe that Carroll's work is not free form, that it has, and seeks, patterns. It is hard to believe that one can still read that Carroll was a kind of improviser, using dream devices as a means to free fantasy, when Gardner long ago showed that the seemingly up-and-down random action in *Through the Looking-Glass*—Alice's constant leaps from square to square and character to character, for example—is a dance made to the logic of a chess problem, so that every lurch of the White Knight has a planned providence in it.

The most important pattern that Gardner finds, or shows, is that tracery of existential dread just visible beneath the poem's surface. Gardner reproduces, in the back matter, F. C. S. Schiller's wonderful pragmatist reading of the *Snark* as a parody of German idealism—of the Hegelian search for the Absolute. And certainly, the absurdity of academic life—of a pursuit of a scarce-known creature by unqualified professionals armed with a blank map—resonates in the poem. Yet Gardner's own more intensely emotive reading, born at the height of the *Dr. Strangelove* time, and drawing on Unamuno and existentialism, is more moving. The Boojum, the unknown thing that the Snark *may* become, is death—or at least the fear of extinction that haunts all conscious living things. The Snarks we pursue, of money and contentment and ambition, still with the Victorian placidity of this peculiar cruise, always turn out to be Boojums. Gardner argues, rightly, that this general dread had become, since 1945, particularized: we live in fear that the current Snark will be the final Boojum, that the society of prosperity in which we live will one morning suddenly vanish away. This reading has a different but equal force now. New York, and indeed America, has, after all, in the years since that fatal morning in 2001, been thoroughly Boojumized. We still hunt Snarks, but each of us is the Baker, the doomed and awkward antihero, with his own private Boojum waiting in the subway or the morning mail. (And never before have we had a Bellman in America with only one notion, and that to tingle his bell.)

But beyond even the depth and current applicability of the poem, all of Gardner's work is important, and worth saving, because, as much as any person can, he has kept alive the practice of catholic imagination. Equally admiring of Chesterton and Russell, he believes, as he has put it in his fine *The Whys of a Philosophical Scrivener*, in "magic," in a personal God, and in much that confounds simple or poverty-stricken or mindless materialism, and at the same time he has been our most untiring pursuer of pseudoscience and irrationality. He is living proof that the space between a feeling heart and a thinking mind, between a love of the marvelous and a reverence for skeptical truth, is a false one; no such line exists, and Chesterton and Shaw can, must, coexist in the mind of anyone trying to make sense of the world. Calling himself a "closet theist," Gardner speaks for all of us who love the imagination of the marvelous and gag on the puerilities of dogmatic religious belief.

This double belief, not contradictory, but nesting imagination within rationality, makes Gardner an ideal commentator on Carroll. Carroll's object of satire is always the folly of pure intellect, the absurdity of trying to figure out life just by thinking about it—yet this is, of course, itself a thought, and one he loves to think about. Skeptical of pure reason, Carroll is never as disgustedly anti-intellectual as Swift. Carroll was above all a poet of the irrational, but he was not an irrationalist. He is one of the greatest of comic writers because he does not see a contradiction, anymore than his annotator does, between what is called logic and what sounds, at first, like lunacy. To understand Carroll in this way—not as a children's writer, of course, not narrowly as a philosopher either, but rather as someone alive to the essential paradox that we live in a world not of our making that our imaginations help to make—is to understand a crucial bit of ourselves.

For we, too, are all Snarks, and are all Boojums. Gardner's belief that everything is miraculous—that experience is amazing, even if the universe is self-made, that the existence of nature as it really is and has evolved is enough wonder to keep the most desperate mystic with his eyes rolling and mouth agape—echoes Carroll's own. It is this double knowledge that sense and nonsense, the world and our wonder at it, coexist that produces poems and readings as mad and good as these.

—April 2006

NEW PREFACE TO
THE ANNOTATED HUNTING
OF THE SNARK

BY MARTIN GARDNER

THE ORIGINAL annotated edition of *The Hunting of the Snark* was published in hardcover in 1962 by Bramhall House, by arrangement with Simon and Schuster. In 1967 Penguin Books, in England, issued a revised paperback, later reprinted with different covers. Both printings featured on their back cover the following jingle:

> The inscrutable 'Snark' leaves us all in the dark . . .
> Is it psocial or filosofycle?
> The dregs from the barrel of Alice's Carroll?
> Or a skit on the whole business cycle?
> Martin Gardner's advice in his notes is concise,
> (Once you've purchased this volume, it's free.)
> He reveals the whole core . . . but we mustn't say more,
> For the Snark was a Boojum, you see.

In 1981 William Kaufmann published a handsome limited edition, signed and numbered, edited by James Tanis and John Dooley, which was followed by a smaller trade edition. Both books contained a wealth of new material and an expanded introduction. In the introduction I mentioned several far-fetched attempts to interpret the *Snark* as an intended allegory. Similar efforts have since been made, the most recent appearing in *The Carrollian*, a journal of England's Lewis Carroll Society, as well as in the American periodical *Knight Letter*. These speculations are closely related to my own contention that Carroll's ballad is an expression of "existential agony" over the inevitability of death.

Fernando Soto, writing on "The Consumption of the Snark" (*The Carrollian*, Autumn 2001), opens his heavily footnoted article by pointing out that the *Snark* was originally published on April Fool's Day, 1876. He believes that this date was deliberately chosen by Carroll and that part of the joke was to falsely and repeatedly insist that he had no ulterior meaning in mind; that his ballad was intended to be pure nonsense, nothing more. For 125 years, Soto is persuaded, the true meaning of the *Snark* was concealed until he, Soto, finally unraveled the mystery.

Shortly before writing the *Snark*, Carroll was deeply distressed by the slow death from tuberculosis of his young cousin and godson Charles Wilcox. Before Charles died, Carroll had been nursing him on the Isle of Wight. The *Snark*, Soto maintains, is a cleverly concealed allegory about consumption. Tuberculosis was then widespread in England, with no known cure. Every member of the ship's crew, Soto argues, is a victim of the dread disease, destined to die when they encounter the Boojum.

Soto calls attention to the *B* that begins the name of each sailor on Carroll's ship. *B* equals *be*. To be or not to be, as Hamlet said, is the question. Soto notes that the *B* of every crew member's name is preceded by *The*. The *T* of *The* is followed by *B*. TB! The Snark is a symbol of consumption, and the Boojum a symbol of death. The ballad, Soto concludes, "must be the most complex allegory ever conceived . . . in my opinion [it] resembles a huge, well-researched, highly complex and symbolic riddle/puzzle impersonating as an April Fool's joke."

Soto does not doubt that the allegory was consciously intended. "Oh, so conscious!" he exclaims. Soto supports this belief with a raft of ingenious correlations. Is he right? I leave it to readers of his paper to decide.

E. Fuller Torrey and Judy Miller, in their article "The Capture of the Snark" (*Knight Letter*, Spring 2004) take a slightly different tack. They argue that instead of the death of Carroll's cousin, the *Snark* reflects the bizarre death of Carroll's much-loved and admired uncle, Robert Wilfred Skeffington Lutwidge. In 1873, when the uncle was visiting the Fisherton Lunatic Asylum in Salisbury, a deranged patient stabbed him in the temple with a large rusty nail. He died at the asylum six days later.

In his diary Carroll recorded the death of his "dear uncle." Torrey and Miller direct the reader to the first line of stanza 6 in Fit 3 of the *Snark*: "A dear uncle of mine (after whom I was named)." Carroll's middle name was Lutwidge, surely the strongest indication that Carroll intended the Baker to be a cartoon of himself. The fit goes on to explain that if the Snark is a Boojum, "You will softly and suddenly vanish away."

Torrey and Miller see the Snark as a symbol of insanity and the Boojum as the crazy, irrational ending of one's life. Each shipmate, they believe, is a lunatic soon to encounter a Boojum. Some members of the crew, the authors speculate, may be based on actual members of the Lunacy Commission that oversaw the asylum. They support their thesis with many ingenious arguments, and finally conclude, in agreement with Soto and myself, that "*The Hunting of the Snark* is not a whimsical nonsense poem"—I would prefer to say not *merely* a nonsense poem—"but rather a cleverly disguised Book of Job."

John S. Kababian called my attention to a sad episode in the life of Dante Rosetti. Addicted to drugs and terminally ill, he became paranoid, convinced that Carroll's *Snark* was a cruel, intended, allegorical attack on himself!

John E. B. Ponsonby sent from England a map of the Andaman Islands, in India's Bay of Bengal. On the map you can see Snark Island. Close to it is Boojum Rock! He and I have no idea how the island and rock got those names.

Carroll later included the *Snark* in his 1883 collection of poems *Rhyme? and Reason?* For a listing of the many changes Carroll made in punctuation, see Selwyn H. Goodacre's "*The Hunting of the Snark*: A History of the Publication" (*Jabberwocky*, Autumn 1976).

—Norman, Oklahoma
May 2006

PREFACE TO

THE CENTENNIAL EDITION
(Kaufmann, 1981)

BY MARTIN GARDNER

ALTHOUGH Lewis Carroll thought of *The Hunting of the Snark* as a nonsense ballad for children, it is hard to imagine—in fact one shudders to imagine—a child of today reading and enjoying it. Victorian children may have found it amusing (there is a grim record of one little girl having recited the entire poem to Carroll during a long carriage ride), but even they, one suspects, were few in number.

"It is not children who ought to read the words of Lewis Carroll," writes Gilbert Chesterton, "they are far better employed making mud-pies." Carroll's nonsense should be read by

> sages and grey-haired philosophers . . . in order to study that darkest problem of metaphysics, the borderland between reason and unreason, and the nature of the most erratic of spiritual forces, humour, which eternally dances between the two. That we do find a pleasure in certain long and elaborate stories, in certain complicated and curious forms of diction, which have no intelligible meaning whatever, is not a subject for children to play with; it is a subject for psychologists to go mad over.[1]

The Hunting of the Snark is a poem over which an unstable, sensitive soul might very well go mad. There is even a touch of madness in the reverse, looking-glass procedure by which it was written. The time was 1874. The Reverend Charles Lutwidge Dodgson, that shy and fastidious bachelor who

---

1. "The Library of the Nursery," in *Lunacy and Letters*, 1958.

taught mathematics at Christ Church, Oxford, was then forty-two and something of a celebrity. He had written two masterpieces that were to immortalize his child-friend, Alice Liddell, and he had published *Phantasmagoria*, a small book of (mostly dull) nonsense poems. On the afternoon of 18 July, in Guilford, the town in Surrey where his sisters lived, Carroll went out for a stroll. This is how he tells the story:

> I was walking on a hillside, alone, one bright summer day, when suddenly there came into my head one line of verse—one solitary line—"For the Snark *was* a Boojum, you see." I knew not what it meant, then: I know not what it means, now; but I wrote it down: and, some time afterwards, the rest of the stanza occurred to me, that being its last line: and so by degrees, at odd moments during the next year or two, the rest of the poem pieced itself together, that being its last stanza.[2]

Carroll first mentioned the poem in his Diary on 23 November 1874 when he showed Ruskin some of the pictures that Henry Holiday had drawn to illustrate the book. He was much disheartened to hear that Ruskin saw no hopes of Holiday doing the work satisfactorily.

Holiday, whom Carroll had first met in Oxford in 1870 and already approached in January 1874 as a possible illustrator of another book, "if *only* he can draw grotesques," was a prominent London painter and sculptor, and later a celebrated designer of stained-glass windows. His autobiography, *Reminiscences of My Life*, reproduces a number of his murals: mostly historical scenes, painted in a classical manner and swarming with nudes and Grecian-robed figures. His stained-glass windows were shipped to churches all over the globe, including dozens in the United States, some in large cities, some in

2. "*Alice* on the Stage," *The Theatre*, April 1887. Morton N. Cohen, in his article "Hark the Snark" (see bibliography), argues convincingly that the ballad's genesis was closely related to Carroll's state of mind during this long and sad vigil in Guildford. Carroll was there to minister to a cousin and godson who was dying of tuberculosis. [I was reminded by Joseph Keogh, a Canadian writer, that Edgar Allan Poe, in his essay "The Philosophy of Composition," said that he began composing *The Raven* by first writing its final lines.]

towns as small as Wappingers Falls, New York, and Thermopolis, Wyoming. His best works, he thought, were the windows—in particular the two huge scenes of the Crucifixion and the Ascension—that he designed and cast for the Church of the Holy Trinity at 316 East Eighty-eighth Street in Manhattan. (They are worth a visit. I sometimes wonder how many of the parishioners, worshipping on Sunday morning, are aware of the fact that these pious patterns of colored glass were designed by the illustrator of *The Hunting of the Snark*.)[3] If anyone had suggested to Holiday that he might be remembered chiefly for his pictures in the *Snark*, or that his autobiography would be collected mainly because of its references to Carroll, he would have been incredulous; as incredulous as Dean Henry George Liddell's official biographer if someone had suggested that among the academic associates of Alice's father, the one destined for the greatest fame was a man nowhere mentioned in the biography!

How well the academician Holiday succeeded in producing grotesques for the *Snark* (it is the only work of Carroll's that he illustrated) is open to debate. Ruskin was certainly right in thinking him inferior to Tenniel. His published drawings are, of course, thoroughly realistic except for the oversize heads and the slightly surrealist quality that derives less from the artist's imagination than from the fact that he was illustrating a surrealist poem.

In his article on "The Snark's Significance" [see p. 107], Holiday tells how the poem came to be illustrated. He describes how Carroll, after he had completed three fits of it, asked for three pictures, and how before they were finished he wrote another fit and asked for another picture, going on, fit after fit, until there were nine pictures in all. One of Holiday's sketches was never used. This is how he explains it:

3. I do not have a complete listing of other churches in Manhattan that have stained-glass windows by Holiday, but I do know of two. The Grace Church, 802 Broadway, has windows depicting Joseph and Benjamin, the four Mary's, the raising of Lazarus, and the raising of the daughter of Jairus. The Church of the Incarnation, Madison Avenue and 35th Street, has windows showing the resurrection and ascension of Jesus, Jacob blessing his children, Jesus commissioning St. Peter, and the Virgin Mary and Dorcas. For a listing of churches in Philadelphia, Chicago, St. Louis, Washington, D.C., and other U.S. cities, for which Holiday designed windows, see the article by Baldry under references on Holiday [in the bibliography].

In our correspondence about the illustrations, the coherence and consistency of the nonsense on its own nonsensical understanding often became prominent. One of the first three I had to do was the disappearance of the Baker, and I not unnaturally invented a Boojum. Mr. Dodgson wrote that it was a delightful monster, but that it was inadmissible. All his descriptions of the Boojum were quite unimaginable, and he wanted the creature to remain so. I assented, of course, though reluctant to dismiss what I am still confident is an accurate representation. I hope that some future Darwin, in a new *Beagle*, will find the beast, or its remains; if he does, I know he will confirm my drawing.

Carroll records in his Diary on 24 October 1875 that he has the sudden notion of publishing the *Snark* as a Christmas poem. But five days later his plan collapses when he hears from Macmillan that it will take at least three months to complete the wood engravings. On 5 November he mentions sending Macmillan the text of three fits. The following day he writes four more stanzas, "completing the poem." On 7 November he sends his "finished" manuscript to Macmillan, but in January of the following year we find him still working on new fits and adding more stanzas to the old ones.

The book was finally published on April 1, 1876, shortly before Easter. This gave Carroll an excuse for inserting into the volume a small pamphlet (later sold separately) entitled *An Easter Greeting* [see p. 73]. He realized that the religious sentiments in this greeting were out of keeping with the ballad, but he may have had a vague, uncomfortable feeling that the gloom and pessimism of his poem needed to be balanced by a reference to the Easter message of hope.

On 29 March Carroll records that he spent six hours at Macmillan inscribing some eighty presentation copies of his book. Many of these inscriptions were acrostic verses on the names of little girls to whom the books were sent.[4] The following two have often been reprinted:

4. One charming acrostic, to Alice Crompton, did not come to light until 1974 when it was reprinted in *The Lewis Carroll Circular*, No. 2, edited by Trevor Winkfield:

Alice dear, will you join me in hunting the Snark?
    Let us go to the chase hand-in-hand:

"ARE you deaf, Father William?" the young man said,
"Did you hear what I told you just now?
"Excuse me for shouting! Don't waggle your head
"Like a blundering, sleepy old cow!
"A little maid dwelling in Wallington Town,
"Is my friend, so I beg to remark:
"Do you think she'd be pleased if a book were sent down
"Entitled 'The Hunt of the Snark'?"

"Pack it up in brown paper!" the old man cried,
"And seal it with olive-and-dove.
"I command you to do it!" he added with pride,
"Nor forget, my good fellow, to send her beside
"Easter Greetings, and give her my love."

MAIDEN, though thy heart may quail
And thy quivering lip grow pale,
Read the Bellman's tragic tale!
Is it life of which it tells?
Of a pulse that sinks and swells
Never lacking chime of bells?
Bells of sorrow, bells of cheer,
Easter, Christmas, glad New Year,

If we only can catch one before it gets dark,
    Could anything happen more grand?

Ever ready to share in the Beaver's despair,
    Count your poor little fingers & thumbs:
Recollecting with tears all the smudges & smears
    On the page where you work at your sums!

May I help you to seek it with thimbles & care?
    Pursuing with forks & hope?
To threaten its life with a railway-share?
Or to charm it with smiles—but a maiden so fair
    Need not trouble herself about soap!

Still they sound, afar, anear.
So may Life's sweet bells for thee,
In the summers yet to be,
Evermore make melody!

Is it life of which it tells? If so, what aspect of life is being told? We know that the *Snark* describes "with infinite humor the impossible voyage of an improbable crew to find an inconceivable creature," as Sidney Williams and Falconer Madan put it in their *Handbook of the Literature of the Rev. C. L. Dodgson*. But is that *all* it describes?

Every serious reader of the *Snark* has pondered this question, and many have tried to answer it. Carroll himself was, of course, asked it repeatedly. On the record, he answered it five times.

1. "Periodically I have received courteous letters from strangers," Carroll wrote in "*Alice* on the Stage," "begging to know whether *The Hunting of the Snark* is an allegory, or contains some hidden moral, or is a political satire: and for all such questions I have but one answer, '*I don't know!*'"

2. In 1876 he wrote to a child-friend: "When you have read the *Snark*, I hope you will write me a little note and tell me how you like it, and if you can *quite* understand it. Some children are puzzled with it. Of course you know what a Snark is? If you do, please tell *me*: for I haven't an idea what it is like. And tell me which of the pictures you like best."

3. This from a letter written in 1880 to a not-so-little girl of nineteen: "I have a letter from you . . . asking me 'Why don't you explain the *Snark*?,' a question I ought to have answered long ago. Let me answer it now—'because I can't.' Are you able to explain things which you don't yourself understand?"

4. In 1896, twenty years after the ballad was published, he is still struggling with the question.

As to the meaning of the *Snark*? [he writes in a long letter to a group of children] I'm very much afraid I didn't mean anything but nonsense! Still, you know, words mean more than we mean to express when we use them: so a whole book ought to mean a great deal more than the writer meant.

So, whatever good meanings are in the book, I'm very glad to accept as the meaning of the book. The best that I've seen is by a lady (she published it in a letter to a newspaper)—that the whole book is an allegory on the search after happiness. I think this fits beautifully in many ways—particularly about the bathing-machines: when the people get weary of life, and can't find happiness in town or in books, then they rush off to the seaside to see what bathing-machines will do for them. [For more on bathing-machines, see note 29, Fit 2, and the illustration on p. 33.]

5. Carroll's last comment on the *Snark* was in a letter written in 1897, a year before his death:

In answer to your question, "What did you mean the Snark was?" will you tell your friend that I meant that the Snark was a *Boojum*. I trust that she and you will now feel quite satisfied and happy.

To the best of my recollection, I had no other meaning in my mind, when I wrote it: but people have since tried to find the meanings in it. The one I like best (which I think is partly my own) is that it may be taken as an allegory for the pursuit of happiness. The characteristic "ambition" works well into this theory—and also its fondness for bathing-machines, as indicating that the pursuer of happiness, when he has exhausted all other devices, betakes himself, as a last and desperate resource, to some such wretched watering-place as Eastbourne, and hopes to find, in the tedious and depressing society of the daughters of mistresses of boarding-schools, the happiness he has failed to find elsewhere. . . .

There is no reason to suppose that Carroll was in the slightest degree evasive in denying that he had intended his poem to mean anything at all. But, as he himself pointed out, words can mean much more than a writer intends. They can express meanings buried so deep in an author's mind that he himself is not aware of them, and they can acquire meanings entirely by accident. Nonsense writing is a peculiarly rich medium for both types of "unintended" meaning.

"I can remember a clever undergraduate at Oxford," writes Holiday in

"The Snark's Significance," "who knew the *Snark* by heart, telling me that on all sorts of occasions, in all the daily incidents of life, some line from the poem was sure to occur to him that exactly fitted. Most people will have noticed this peculiarity of Lewis Carroll's writing." When a Carrollian nonsense line suggests one of these neat metaphorical applications, who can say, particularly in the case of the *Snark*, whether the fit is fortuitous or whether it derives from a level below the Fit—that dark, unconscious substratum of intent that underlies all great creative acts?

Many attempts have been made to force the whole of the *Snark* into one overall metaphorical pattern. A writer with the initials M.H.T., in a note appended to Holiday's article on the ballad's significance, argues that the Snark represents material wealth. "I am always lost in astonishment," he says, "at the people who think it can be anything else. Observe the things with which its capture was attempted. Why, the mere mention of railway shares and soap is sufficient of itself to establish my thesis." The Boojum, according to this writer, is that type of unexpected good fortune that lifts a man "into a sphere in which he is miserable, and makes his wife cut the greengrocer's lady."

A second note to Holiday's article, this one signed St. J.E.C.H., takes the position that the poem is a satire on the craving for social advancement, the tragedy of the person who tries to climb into society but never gets higher on the ladder than the local Browning club.

Two events that took place at the time Carroll's ballad was being written gave rise to two popular theories about the poem. One event was the famous trial of the Tichborne claimant, discussed in note 54 [now note 57, Fit 6]. The other was an arctic expedition on two steamships, the *Alert* and *Discovery*, that set out from Portsmouth in 1875, returning in the fall of 1876. The expedition was much in the news before and after the publication of the *Snark*, and many readers apparently supposed that the ballad was a satire on an arctic voyage, the Snark a symbol of the North Pole. There is little to recommend this theory, although the polar expedition, like the Tichborne case, undoubtedly added to the topical interest of the poem.

A theory closely related to the material-wealth theory of M.H.T. was proposed in 1911 by Devereux Court in an article in the *Cornhill Magazine*. Court thought that the poem satirized an unsound business venture. The ship's company is the business company. The vessel has been "floated." The men on board are the men on the company's board of directors, all of them speculators fond of "quotations." The Bellman is the chairman of the board, the Boots the secretary. The Snark is a land shark who brings about the company's downfall.

The latest variant of this interpretation was advanced in the early thirties by Dean Wallace B. Donham of the Harvard Graduate School of Business Administration. His views are defended at length in an article, "Finding of the Snark," by Arthur Ruhl, in the *Saturday Review of Literature*, 18 March 1933. Dean Donham's opinion is that the Snark is a satire on business in general, the Boojum a symbol of a business slump, and the whole thing a tragedy about the business cycle. In 1933 the United States was of course in the midst of the great depression. The poem's allegorical level is worked out with considerable ingenuity: the Boots is unskilled labor, the Beaver is a textile worker, the Baker a small businessman in a luxury trade, the Billiard-marker a speculator, the hyenas are stockbrokers, the bear is a stock market bear, the Jubjub is Disraeli, and so on. The Bandersnatch, who keeps snatching at the Banker in Fit 7, is the Bank of England, repeatedly raising its interest rate in the wild optimism that preceded the panic of 1875. It was Dean Donham's belief that "no single quatrain in the *Snark* goes contra to the interpretation," but the reader will have to consult Ruhl's article for a fuller defense of that statement.

The most elaborate and witty of all Snark theories is the tongue-in-cheek concoction of the philosopher Ferdinand Canning Scott Schiller. Schiller is almost forgotten today, but at the turn of the century he was recognized, along with William James and John Dewey, as one of the three principal leaders of the pragmatic movement. Schiller had a zest for logical paradoxes, practical jokes, and outrageous puns. (He would have made a sterling member of the Snark hunting crew, under the name of the Bachelor; he managed to avoid marrying until he was seventy-one.) In 1901, when he was teaching philosophy at Oxford, he persuaded the editors of *Mind*, a philosophical journal, to bring out a parody issue. Schiller's "A Commentary on the *Snark*," for which he used the pseudonym of Snarkophilus Snobbs, is the highlight of this issue. It interprets Carroll's ballad as a satire on the Hegelian philosopher's search for the Absolute. The full text of this commentary will be found in the appendix of this section, so I shall say no more about it here [see p. 80].

Is there more to be said about the *Snark*? Yes, there is yet another way of looking at the poem, an existentialist way if you will, that for several reasons is singularly appropriate to our time.

The key to this interpretation is in the last five stanzas of Fit 3. The Baker's uncle, perhaps on his deathbed, has just informed the Baker that if the Snark he confronts turns out to be a Boojum, he will "softly and suddenly vanish away, and never be met with again!" In the next four stanzas the Baker describes his emotional reaction to this solemn warning. In keeping with the Bellman's rule-of-three, he says it three times to underscore the truth of what he is saying. He is in a state of acute existential nausea.

> "It is this, it is this that oppresses my soul,
>   When I think of my uncle's last words:
> And my heart is like nothing so much as a bowl
>   Brimming over with quivering curds!"

This existential anxiety, as the existential analysts like to call it (earlier ages called it simply the fear of death), is of course a thoroughly normal emotion. But, for one reason or another, both individuals and cultures vary widely in the degree to which they suppress this emotion. Until recently, at least in England and the United States, death as a natural process had become almost unmentionable. As Geoffrey Gorer puts it in his article on "The Pornography of Death,"[5] one of the peculiar features of our time is that while violent death, and the possibility of violent death, has greatly increased, and while it plays an "ever-growing part in the fantasies offered to mass audiences—detective stories, thrillers, Westerns, war stories, spy stories, science fiction, and eventually horror comics," talk about natural death has become "more and more smothered in prudery." It is the great conversation stopper of parlor discourse.

---

5. *Encounter*, October 1955. Since this appeared "thanatology" has received increasing attention as a topic of both public and academic interest.

Lewis Carroll lived in a different age, an age in which death was domesticated and sentimentalized, an age in which readers were able to weep real tears over the passing of Dickens's Little Nell. Carroll thought a great deal about death and, I am persuaded, about the possibility of his own nonexistence. Jokes about death abound in his writings, even in the *Alice* books. His rejection of the doctrine of eternal punishment was his one major departure from Protestant orthodoxy. In the introduction to his book *Pillow Problems* he speaks of the value of mental work at night in keeping one's mind free of unholy thoughts. "There are sceptical thoughts, which seem for the moment to uproot the firmest faith; there are blasphemous thoughts, which dart unbidden into the most reverent souls; there are unholy thoughts, which torture with their hateful presence, the fancy that would fain be pure."

I believe that Carroll is describing here a state of existential dread. I think it is what he had in mind, perhaps not consciously, when he has the Baker say:

"I engage with the Snark—every night after dark—
    In a dreamy delirious fight:
I serve it with greens in those shadowy scenes,
    And I use it for striking a light."

Its use for striking a light—the light of faith—is the central theme of Miguel de Unamuno's great existential work, *The Tragic Sense of Life*. Scores of books have been written in the past few decades about the existentialist movement, but for some impenetrable reason most of them do not even mention Unamuno, the Spanish poet, novelist, and philosopher (he died in 1936) whose outlook is certainly closer to Kierkegaard's than that of many philosophers who wear the existentialist label. The Baker's remarks about his uncle's last words are a metaphorical compression of scores of passages that can be found in Unamuno's writings. Here is a moving example from his commentary on *Don Quixote*:

. . . one of those moments when the soul is blown about by a sudden gust from the wings of the angel of mystery. A moment of anguish. For there are times when, unsuspecting, we are suddenly seized, we know not how nor whence, by a vivid sense of our mortality, which takes us without warning and quite unprepared. When most absorbed in the cares and duties of life, or engrossed and self-forgetful on some festal occasion or engaged in a pleasant chat, suddenly it seems that death is fluttering over me. Not death, something worse, a sensation of annihilation, a supreme anguish. And this anguish, tearing us violently from our perception of appearances, with a single stunning swoop, dashes us away—to recover into an awareness of the substance of things.

All creation is something we are some day to lose, and is some day to lose us. For what else is it to vanish from the world but the world vanishing from us? Can you conceive of yourself as not existing? Try it. Concentrate your imagination on it. Fancy yourself without vision, hearing, the sense of touch, the ability to perceive anything. Try it. Perhaps you will evoke and bring upon yourself that anguish which visits us when least expected; perhaps you will feel the hangman's knot choking off your soul's breath. Like the woodpecker in the oak tree, an agony is busily pecking at our hearts, to make its nest there.

It is this agony, the agony of anticipating one's loss of being, that pecks at the heart of Carroll's poem. Did he realize that *B*, the dominant letter of his ballad, is a symbol of "be"? I sometimes think he did. At any rate, the letter sounds through the poem like a continuous drum beat, starting softly with the introduction of the Bellman, the Boots, and the others, then growing more and more insistent until, in a final thunderclap, it becomes the Boojum.

The *Snark* is a poem about being and nonbeing, an existential poem, a poem of existential agony. The Bellman's map is the map that charts the course of humanity; blank because we possess no information about where we are or whither we drift.[6] The ship's bowsprit gets mixed with its rudder and when we

---

6. "If thought of as isolated in the midst of the ocean, a ship can stand for mankind and human society moving through time and struggling with its destiny. . . . *The Hunting of the Snark* is a pure example of [this] use. . . ."—W. H. Auden, *The Enchafed Flood.*

think we sail west we sail east. The Snark is, in Paul Tillich's fashionable phrase, every man's ultimate concern. This is the great search motif of the poem, the quest for an ultimate good. But this motif is submerged in a stronger motif, the dread, the agonizing dread, of ultimate failure. The Boojum is more than death. It is the end of all searching. It is final, absolute extinction, in Auden's phrase, "the dreadful Boojum of Nothingness." In a literal sense, Carroll's Boojum means nothing at all. It is the void, the great blank emptiness out of which we miraculously emerged; by which we will ultimately be devoured; through which the absurd galaxies spiral and drift endlessly on their nonsense voyages from nowhere to nowhere.[7]

Perhaps you are a naturalist and humanist, or a Sartrean existentialist. You believe passionately in working for a better world, and although you know that you will not be around to enjoy it, you take a kind of comfort—poor substitute that it is!—from the fact that future generations, perhaps even your own children, may reap the rewards of your labors. But what if they won't? Atomic energy is a Snark that comes in various shapes and sizes. A certain number of intercontinental guided missiles—the U.S. Air Force has one it calls the Snark—with thermonuclear warheads can glide gently down on the just and unjust, and the whole of humanity may never be met with again.

For the Snark was a. . . .

We are poised now on the brink of discovering the unsuspected meaning that Carroll's poem acquired in 1942 when Enrico Fermi and his associates (working, appropriately, in a former "squash" court) obtained the first sustained nuclear chain reaction.

Consider for a moment that remarkable four-letter word *bomb*. It begins and ends with *b*. The second *b* is silent; the final silence. B for birth, non-*b* for Nothing. Between the two *b*'s (to be or not to be) is *Om*, Hindu symbol for the

---

7. There is no evidence that Carroll ever read *Moby-Dick*, but more than one critic has found parallels between Melville's novel and Carroll's ballad. No one has discussed the parallels more fully or more profoundly than Harold Beaver (author of an annotated *Moby-Dick*) in his essay "Whale or Boojum" (see bibliography). At the top of his essay he quotes the following passage from Melville's chapter on whiteness: "Is it that by its indefiniteness it shadows forth the heartless voids and immensities of the universe, and thus stabs us from behind with the thought of annihilation, when beholding the white depths of the milky way?"

nature of Brahman, the Absolute, the god behind the lesser gods whose tasks are to create, preserve, and destroy all that is.

"I believe it [the atom bomb] is the greatest of all American inventions," declared H. L. Mencken, "and one of the imperishable glories of Christianity. It surpasses the burning of heretics on all counts, but especially on the count that it has given the world an entirely new disease, to wit, galloping carcinoma."[8] This disease advanced to a new stage in August 1961, when Khrushchev announced that the Soviet Union would unilaterally resume nuclear testing, perhaps build a 100-megaton bomb. A political cartoon in the *Boston Traveler* showed Khrushchev sticking his head around a corner, a cloud mushrooming from his mouth and bearing the single word "BOO." No Snarxist need be told "the word he was trying to say."

A bookish pastime, recommended for whiling away the hours left to us in these tropical climes of cancer, is that of searching odd corners of literature for passages unintentionally prophetic of the Bomb. Here, for example, is Vincent Starrett's poem "Portent."[9]

> "Heavy, heavy—over thy head—"
>   Hear them call in the room below!
> Now they patter with gruesome tread,
>   Now they riot with laugh and blow.
>   Tchk! What a pity that they must grow!
> "Heavy, heavy—over thy head—"
>
> "Heavy, heavy—over thy head—"
>   Winds are bleak as they coil and blow.
> Once the sky was a golden red;
>   Once I played in that room below.
>   Sometimes I think that children know!
> "Heavy, heavy—over thy head—"

8. As quoted in *Life*, 5 August 1946.
9. From *Flame and Dust*, 1924.

Paul Goodman's novel *The Grand Piano* (1941) closes with its hero, Horatio Alger, wiring an explosive to the piano key of B flat (Carroll's B again!) just below the center of the keyboard. The idea is to play a composition in which the tones cluster around the death note, never touching it, but always calling for it as a resolution.

This is, of course, precisely the wild, demonic music that the U.S. and the U.S.S.R. have been playing, and in which other, less skillful musicians are joining. It is this background music that gives to Lewis Carroll's poem, when it is read today, a new dimension of anxiety. The Baker is Man himself, on the Brink, erect, sublime, wagging his head like an idiot, cackling with laughter and glee.

Suddenly that startled, choked-off cry, "It's a Boo—"

Then silence. . . .

Perhaps otherwise. Perhaps the Bomb will prove to be not a Boojum but only a harmless variety of Snark. The human race will continue to creep onward and upward, stretching out its hands, as H. G. Wells liked to say, to the stars. Take comfort from such happy thoughts, you who can. The Boojum remains. Like T. S. Eliot's eternal Footman, it snickers at the coattails of every member of humanity's motley crew.

> Twilight and evening bell,
> And after that the Snark!

These lines could serve as a caption for the poem's final illustration. Beyond the craggy precipice, in the shadows of a terrible twilight, a man of flesh and bone is vanishing. Send not to know, dear reader, for whom the Bellman's bell tolls.

FIRST EDITION COVERS
BY HENRY HOLIDAY

THE two pages that follow repro-
duce the spine and front and back
covers of the *Snark's* first edition. Note
that the front cover depicts a bell*man*,
and the back cover depicts a bell*bouy*.

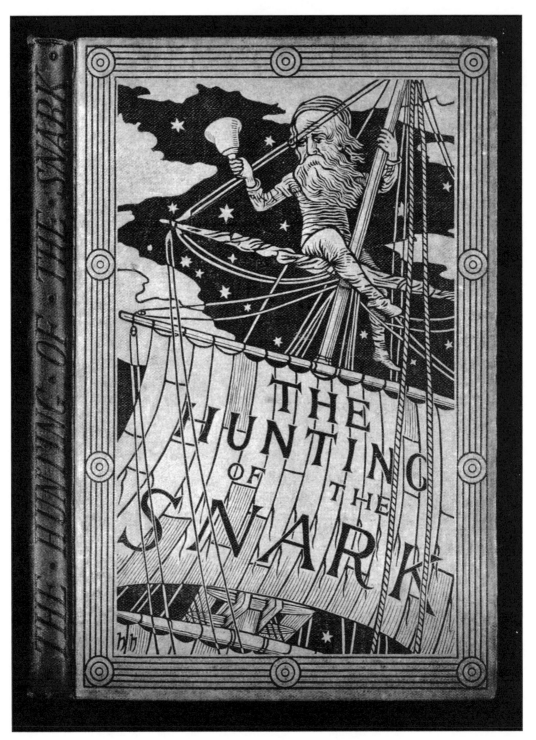

Spine and front cover of the first edition of the *Snark*.

Back cover of the first edition of the *Snark*.

THE HUNTING OF THE SNARK

An Agony in Eight Fits

Inscribed to a dear Child:
in memory of golden summer hours
and whispers of a summer sea.[1]

GIRT with a boyish garb for boyish task,
    Eager she wields her spade: yet loves as well
Rest on a friendly knee, intent to ask
      The tale he loves to tell.[2]

Rude spirits of the seething outer strife,
    Unmeet to read her pure and simple spright,
Deem, if you list, such hours a waste of life,
      Empty of all delight!

Chat on, sweet Maid, and rescue from annoy
    Hearts that by wiser talk are unbeguiled.
Ah, happy he who owns that tenderest joy,
      The heart-love of a child!

Away, fond thoughts, and vex my soul no more!
    Work claims my wakeful nights, my busy days—
Albeit bright memories of that sunlit shore
      Yet haunt my dreaming gaze!

1. Of the many acrostics that Lewis Carroll wrote for his child-friends, this is perhaps the most ingenious. Not only do the initial letters of the lines spell Gertrude Chataway, but her name is also indicated by the first words of each stanza: *Girt, Rude, Chat, Away.* A similar letter/syllable acrostic is Carroll's dedicatory poem to Isa Bowman in the first volume of *Sylvie and Bruno.*

Carroll made friends with hundreds of little girls, but there were several of whom he was particularly fond and who received more than his usual attention. The first and most intense of these special friendships was, of course, with Alice Liddell, the original of his fictional Alice.

Gertrude was the second. He first met her in 1875 on the beach at Sandown, a small bathing resort. She was with her parents and three sisters. Gertrude was then almost eight. This is how she later recalled the occasion (from *The Life and Letters of Lewis Carroll*, by Stuart Dodgson Collingwood):

"I first met Mr. Lewis Carroll on the sea-shore at Sandown in the Isle of Wight, in the summer of 1875, when I was quite a little child.

"We had all been taken there for change of air, and next door there was an old gentleman—to me at any rate he seemed old—who interested me immensely. He would come on to his balcony, which joined ours, sniffing the sea-air with his head thrown back, and would walk right down the steps on to the beach with his chin in air, drinking in the fresh breezes as if he could never have enough. I do not know why this excited such keen curiosity on my part, but I remember well that whenever I heard his footstep I flew out to see him coming, and when one day he spoke to me my joy was complete.

"Thus we made friends, and in a very little while I was as familiar with the interior of his lodgings as with our own.

"I had the usual child's love for fairy-tales and marvels, and his power of telling stories naturally fascinated me. We used to sit for hours on the wooden steps which led from our garden on to the beach, whilst he told the most lovely tales that could possibly be imagined, often illustrating the exciting situations with a pencil as he went along.

"One thing that made his stories particularly charming to a child was that he often took his cue from her remarks—a question would set him off on quite a new trail of ideas, so that one felt that one had somehow helped to make the story, and it seemed a personal possession. It was the most lovely nonsense conceivable, and I naturally reveled in it. His vivid imagination would fly from one subject to another, and was never tied down in any way by the probabilities of life.

"To *me* it was of course all perfect, but it is astonishing that *he* never seemed either tired or to want other society. I spoke to him once of this since I have been grown up, and he told me it was the greatest pleasure he could have to converse freely with a child, and feel the depths of her mind.

"He used to write to me and I to him after that summer, and the friendship, thus begun, lasted. His letters were one of the greatest joys of my childhood.

"I don't think that he ever really understood that we, whom he had known as children, could not always remain such. I stayed with him only a few years ago, at Eastbourne, and felt for the time

that I was once more a child. He never appeared to realize that I had grown up, except when I reminded him of the fact and then he only said, 'Never mind: you will always be a child to me, even when your hair is grey.'"

A pencil sketch and a photograph that Carroll made of Gertrude, wearing her "boyish garb," are reproduced opposite p. 476 in *The Letters of Lewis Carroll*, edited by Morton N. Cohen with the assistance of Roger Lancelyn Green, and the sketch is also reproduced here. Carroll's friendships with little girls usually cooled when they reached adolescence, but Gertrude was an exception. When she was twenty-five he wrote her an affectionate letter, recalling "like a dream of fifty years ago" the "little bare-legged girl in a sailor's jersey, who used to run up into my lodgings by the sea." In his Diary Carroll notes on 19 September 1893 that Gertrude (then almost twenty-seven) arrived for a visit at his lodging in Eastbourne. The next entry, four days later, is: "Gertrude left. It has been a really delightful visit" (*Lewis Carroll's Diaries*, ed. Roger L. Green, 1953).

It was this visit, Roger Green discloses in his commentary on the Diary, that prompted a letter from Carroll's sister, raising the question of whether it was proper for him to permit young ladies, unescorted, to visit him at the seaside. Carroll's reply, quoted from *The Letters*, is characteristic:

". . . I think all you say about my girl-guests is most kind and sisterly, . . . But I don't think it at all advisable to enter into any controversy about it. There is no reasonable probability that it would modify the views either of you or of me. I will say a few words to explain my views: but I have no wish whatever to have 'the last word': so please say anything you like afterwards.

"You and your husband have, I think, been very fortunate to know so little, by experience, in your own case or in that of your friends, of the wicked recklessness with which people repeat things to the disadvantage of others, without a thought as to whether they have grounds for asserting what they say. I have met with a good deal of utter misrepresentation of that kind. And another result of my experience is the conviction that the opinion of 'people' in general is absolutely worthless as a test of right and wrong. The only two tests I now apply to such a question as the having some particular girl-friend as a guest are, first, my own *conscience*, to settle whether I feel it to be entirely innocent and right, in the sight of God; secondly, the *parents* of my friend, to settle whether I have their *full* approval

Pencil sketch by Lewis Carroll of Gertrude Chataway at the seaside.

for what I do. You need not be shocked at my being spoken against. *Anybody*, who is spoken about at all, is *sure* to be spoken against by *somebody*: and any action, however innocent in itself, is liable, and not at all unlikely, to be blamed by *somebody*. If you limit your actions in life to things that *nobody* can possibly find fault with, you will not do much!"

When Carroll completed his acrostic poem to Gertrude, about a month after first meeting her, he mailed a copy to Mrs. Chataway with a request for permission to print it some day. Evidently she did not notice the concealed name because after hearing from her, Carroll wrote again to call her attention to the double acrostic and to ask if this made any difference in the permission she had given. "If I print them," he wrote, "I shan't tell anyone it is an acrostic—but someone will be sure to find it out before long."

Ten days later he wrote again to tell Gertrude's mother of his plans to use the poem as a dedication in his forthcoming book, *The Hunting of the Snark*. "The scene is laid," he writes, "in an island frequented by the Jubjub and Bandersnatch—no doubt the very island in which the Jabberwock was slain."

2. In Carroll's first version of this poem, as he sent it to Gertrude's mother for approval (see *A Selection from the Letters of Lewis Carroll to His Child-friends*), the last two lines of the first stanza read:

> Rest on a friendly knee, the tale to ask
> That he delights to tell.

A third version of the poem, with minor alterations, appears as the inscription of Carroll's book of poems, *Rhyme? and Reason?*

PREFACE

BY LEWIS CARROLL

IF—and the thing is wildly possible—the charge of writing nonsense were ever brought against the author of this brief but instructive poem, it would be based, I feel convinced, on the line,

"Then the bowsprit got mixed with the rudder sometimes."

In view of this painful possibility, I will not (as I might) appeal indignantly to my other writings as a proof that I am incapable of such a deed: I will not (as I might) point to the strong moral purpose of this poem itself, to the arithmetical principles so cautiously inculcated in it, or to its noble teachings in Natural History—I will take the more prosaic course of simply explaining how it happened.

The Bellman, who was almost morbidly sensitive about appearances, used to have the bowsprit unshipped once or twice a week to be revarnished, and it more than once happened, when the time came for replacing it, that no one on board could remember which end of the ship it belonged to. They knew it was not of the slightest use to appeal to the Bellman about it—he would only refer to his Naval Code, and read out in pathetic tones Admiralty Instructions which none of them had ever been able to understand—so it generally ended in its being fastened on, anyhow, across the rudder. The helmsman* used to stand by with tears in his eyes: *he* knew it was all wrong, but alas! Rule 42 of

---

* This office was usually undertaken by the Boots, who found in it a refuge from the Baker's constant complaints about the insufficient blacking of his three pair of boots.

the Code, "*No one shall speak to the Man at the Helm,*" had been completed by the Bellman himself with the words "*and the Man at the Helm shall speak to no one.*" So remonstrance was impossible, and no steering could be done till the next varnishing day. During these bewildering intervals the ship usually sailed backwards.

As this poem is to some extent connected with the lay of the Jabberwock, let me take this opportunity of answering a question that has often been asked me, how to pronounce "slithy toves." The "i" in "slithy" is long, as in "writhe"; and "toves" is pronounced so as to rhyme with "groves." Again, the first "o" in "borogoves" is pronounced like the "o" in "borrow." I have heard people try to give it the sound of the "o" in "worry." Such is Human Perversity.

This also seems a fitting occasion to notice the other hard words in that poem. Humpty-Dumpty's theory, of two meanings packed into one word like a portmanteau, seems to me the right explanation for all.

For instance, take the two words "fuming" and "furious." Make up your mind that you will say both words, but leave it unsettled which you will say first. Now open your mouth and speak. If your thoughts incline ever so little towards "fuming," you will say "fuming-furious"; if they turn, by even a hair's breadth, towards "furious," you will say "furious-fuming"; but if you have that rarest of gifts, a perfectly balanced mind, you will say "frumious."

Supposing that, when Pistol uttered the well-known words—

"Under which king, Bezonian? Speak or die!"

Justice Shallow had felt certain that it was either William or Richard, but had not been able to settle which, so that he could not possibly say either name before the other, can it be doubted that, rather than die, he would have gasped out "Rilchiam!"

The Landing.

3. *Agony* is here used in the old sense of a struggle that involves great anguish, bodily pain, or death. Carroll also may have had in mind the "woeful agony" that periodically seizes Coleridge's Ancient Mariner, forcing him to tell to strangers his "ghastly tale."

Fit has the double meaning of a convulsion and a canto. *The Oxford English Dictionary* quotes Samuel Johnson: "A long ballad in many fits," and Lord Byron: "one fytte of Harold's pilgrimage." Phyllis Greenacre, in her psychoanalytical study of Carroll (*Swift and Carroll*, 1955), thinks there is some connection between the fact that Carroll's poem has eight fits and Carroll had eight younger siblings.

Carroll had once before punned on the word *fit*. In *Alice's Adventures in Wonderland*, during the trial of the Knave of Hearts, the King quotes the poetic line "*before she had this fit.*" "You never had *fits*, my dear, I think?" he asks his wife. When she replies "Never!" the King says, "Then the words don't *fit* you." This produces dead silence in the courtroom.

THE HUNTING
OF THE SNARK

An Agony in Eight Fits[3]

Fit the First

THE LANDING

"JUST the place for a Snark!"[4] the Bellman[5] cried,
　　As he landed his crew with care;
Supporting each man on the top of the tide
　　By a finger entwined in his hair.[6]

"Just the place for a Snark! I have said it twice:
　　That alone should encourage the crew.
Just the place for a Snark! I have said it thrice:
　　What I tell you three times is true."[7]

4. Beatrice Hatch, in her article "Lewis Carroll" (*Strand Magazine*, April 1898, pp. 413–23), says that Carroll once told her that *Snark* was a portmanteau word for *snail* and *shark*; but "one suspects," writes Phyllis Greenacre in *Swift and Carroll*, "that snake has crept into this portmanteau." Stephen Barr, a correspondent in Woodstock, N.Y., suggests *snarl* and *bark* as another pair of meanings that may be packed together here.

Joseph Keogh wrote from Ontario, Canada, to inform me that *Snark* is an old Germanic word that actually conveys a method by which the beast could be captured! According to Skeat's *Concise Etymological Dictionary* (1882), *Snark*, like the current word *snare*, derives from three Aryan roots: (1) *sna*, meaning "bind together; fasten with string or twine"; (2) *snar*, "to twist, draw tight"; and (3) *snark*, "to twist, entwine, make a noose." *Snark*, Skeat adds, also means "bathe, swim, float" (i.e., like a shark?). It is not known if Carroll was aware of these old Aryan roots.

5. *Bellman* is another word for a town crier. The Bellman is, of course, the captain of the ship and the man who organized the Snark hunt. On early ships a bell would be struck every half hour to indicate the number of half hours that had elapsed in each four-hour watch, so perhaps this is one of the Bellman's chores. Perhaps, also, there is a connection between the agony's eight fits and the fact that eight bells marked the end of a watch.

Contemporary readers fancied a resemblance to Tennyson in Holiday's pictures of the Bellman.

The Bellman appears, whole or in part, in every illustration except the one of the Butcher sharpening his hatchet.

In *Lewis Carroll: A Biography*, Anne Clarke reports that the Oxford University Statutes, which Carroll swore to uphold during his matriculation ceremony at Christ Church, provided for an officer called Le Bellman, or the "ringer." Whenever an important university person died, the bellman's duty was to give notice of the burial by going about ringing a handbell. Because the Snark hunt proved fatal to the Baker, Ms. Clark argues plausibly that Carroll may have had this officer in mind when he included a bellman among the ship's crew.

6. The crew member shown supported by his hair in Holiday's illustration for this stanza is the Banker. He is carrying a telescope (see Fit 5, note 47). The word *Swain* in the lower right corner is the surname of Joseph Swain, the man who made the wood engravings from Holiday's original drawings.

7. The Bellman's rule-of-three is invoked later (Fit 5) to establish the presence of the Jubjub, though the Beaver has considerable difficulty making sure that three statements have in fact occurred. Norbert Wiener, in his classic book *Cybernetics* (New York: J. Wiley, 1948), pointed out that answers given by a computer are often checked by asking the computer to solve the same problem several times, or by giving the problem to several different computers. Wiener speculated on whether the human brain contains a similar checking mechanism: "We can hardly expect that any important message is entrusted for transmission to a single neuron, nor that any important operation is entrusted to a single neuronal mechanism. Like the computing machine, the brain probably works on a variant of the famous principle expounded by Lewis Carroll in *The Hunting of the Snark*: 'What I tell you three times is true.' "

Another mathematician said it this way in the preface to his *Introduction to Matrix Analysis* (New York: McGraw-Hill, 1970). "The human mind

being what it is, repetition and cross-sections from different angles are powerful pedagogical devices. In this connection, it is appropriate to quote Lewis Carroll in *The Hunting of the Snark*, Fit the First—'I have said it thrice: What I tell you three times is true'—The Bellman." And who was the author of this textbook? Richard Bellman!

In arithmetic, an ancient rule for calculating ratios was well known in Carroll's day as the rule-of-three. Carroll refers to it in the dedicatory poem of *A Tangled Tale*, and the Mad Gardener's song in *Sylvie and Bruno* also mentions it:

> He thought he saw a Garden-Door
> That opened with a key:
> He looked again, and found it was
> A Double Rule of Three:
> "And all its mystery," he said,
> "Is clear as day to me!"

Carroll's quite different rule-of-three plays a central role in the plot of a bizarre science-fiction story, "Chaos, Coordinated," by John MacDougal (pseudonym of Robert Lowndes and James Blish). The earth is at war with a distant galaxy, where the various races are coordinated by a gigantic computer. An earthman manages to disguise *The Hunting of the Snark* as an "observational report" and feed it to the giant brain. The brain accepts literally the order "What I tell you three times is true." All it had been told once or twice in the past is regarded as unverified, and new observational reports are not accepted because they are made only once. As a result the entire galaxy becomes, so to speak, snarked. The machine issues blank star maps, distributes bells to spaceship captains, stocks medical chests with muffins, ice, mustard and cress, jam, two volumes of proverbs, and a recording of riddles beginning with "Why is a raven like a writing desk?" (see Fit 3, stanza 1). The story appeared in the magazine *Astounding Science Fiction*, October 1946.

The American writer Edith Wharton was fond of the *Snark* when she was a little girl. In her

> The crew was complete: it included a Boots—8
>   A maker of Bonnets and Hoods—
> A Barrister, brought to arrange their disputes—
>   And a Broker,9 to value their goods.
>
> A Billiard-marker,10 whose skill was immense,
>   Might perhaps have won more than his share—
> But a Banker, engaged at enormous expense,11
>   Had the whole of their cash in his care.

autobiography, *A Backward Glance* (New York: D. Appleton-Century, 1934), pp. 311–2, she tells of a lunch with President Theodore Roosevelt, whom she had known since her childhood. "Well," he said, "I *am* glad to welcome to the White House someone to whom I can quote *The Hunting of the Snark* without being asked what I mean! . . . Would you believe it, no one in the administration has ever heard of Alice, much less of the Snark, and the other day, when I said to the Secretary of Navy: 'Mr. Secretary, *What I say three times is true*,' he did not recognize the allusion, and answered with an aggrieved air: 'Mr. President, it would never for a moment have occurred to me to impugn your veracity!' "

8. A "boots" is a servant at a hotel or inn, formerly assigned to such low tasks as cleaning boots and brushing clothes. No one knows what the Boots looks like; he is the one crew member who does not appear in any of Holiday's illustrations.

Abigail and Gregory Acland, writing on " 'The Crew Was Complete: . . . ,' But How Many Was That?" in *Jabberwocky* (Winter 1992–93) defend a startling conjecture. They suggest that there are only nine members of the ship's crew, not ten, because the Boots is also the maker of bonnets and hoods! This would, of course, explain why Holiday did not include a picture of Boots.

Bonnets and hoods, the authors disclose, are nautical terms. They quote a dictionary definition of *bonnet* as "an additional piece of canvas laced to the foot of a jib or foresail." *Hood* is a naval term for any canvas covering of a hatch, skylight, or the "eyes" of rigging to keep water from damaging them. Boots and the Bonnet-maker seem to be two persons in Fit 4, but the Aclands have ways of getting around this. They make no comment on Holiday's picture of the Bonnet-maker holding a lady's bonnet.

9. Not a pawnbroker, but one licensed to appraise and sell household goods. When a landlord took possession of the furniture of those unable to pay rent, the broker would be called in to "value their goods." Anti-Semitic caricatures of such brokers, with bowler hats and Disraeli sidelocks, were common in the cartoons of Victorian England, and in novels and plays. "People hate and scout 'em," wrote Dickens, "because they're the ministers of wretchedness, like, to poor people" (*Sketches by Boz*, chapter 5.)

Because so many brokers in Carroll's day were Jewish, Holiday took it upon himself to give the Broker an ugly face worthy of a Nazi poster. He had a large nose, thick lips, a monocle, and long flowing locks. Carroll objected strongly to the caricature and insisted that Holiday substitute a less objectionable portrait.

Note, however, that much of the initial caricature survives in the Broker's head in the upper left corner of Holiday's picture of "The Hunting" (p. 43).

Holiday's original drawings are reproduced in

the Kaufmann edition along with a marvelously detailed history of Holiday's work by Charles Mitchell in which he calls attention to the many differences between original sketches and the final engravings by Joseph Swain, which are reproduced in the book you hold. Many of Holiday's preliminary sketches are owned by Princeton University's library and are reproduced in the Kaufmann edition, including a lovely sketch of Hope as a full-figured nude.

10. A "billiard-marker" is the employee of a billiard parlor who keeps a record of the game by marking the points made by each player.

I like to think that the crew's Billiard-marker is none other than the billiard-marker whom Sherlock Holmes and his brother Mycroft observed, many years later, strolling down Pall Mall with his friend the Boots. After leaving the Bellman's crew, the Boots had enlisted in the Royal Artillery. He was discharged after honorable service in India, but was so fond of his boots that he continued to wear them (as Mycroft noticed) after his retirement from service. (See the story of "The Greek Interpreter" in *Memoirs of Sherlock Holmes*. For the friendship between Holmes and Carroll, see William S. Baring-Gould, *Sherlock Holmes of Baker Street*, (New York: C. N. Potter, 1962, pp. 26–7.)

11. I am indebted to correspondent Wilfred H. Shepherd for telling me that "engaged at enormous expense" was, and still is, a ritual phrase used by masters of ceremony in British music halls when they introduce the star of the show. The syllable "nor" in "enormous" is heavily accented, and the audience joins in reciting the entire phrase. "The effect," writes Shepherd, "is much like that of a breaking wave, and as inexplicably pleasant to the ear."

The Crew On Board.

There was also a Beaver, that paced on the deck,
  Or would sit making lace in the bow:
And had often (the Bellman said) saved them from wreck,
  Though none of the sailors knew how.

There was one who was famed for the number of things
  He forgot when he entered the ship:
His umbrella, his watch, all his jewels and rings,
  And the clothes he had bought for the trip.

He had forty-two boxes, all carefully packed,
  With his name painted clearly on each:[12]
But, since he omitted to mention the fact,
  They were all left behind on the beach.

The loss of his clothes hardly mattered, because
  He had seven coats on when he came,
With three pair of boots—but the worst of it was,
  He had wholly forgotten his name.[13]

12. Five of these forty-two boxes can be observed through the window in the illustration of the Baker and his uncle (see p. 40); unfortunately the picture is not clear enough to make out the name painted on two of the boxes. For the meaning of these boxes and the probable name of their owner, see Fit 3, note 34. Observe, in the picture of the Baker on the upper deck, that he is sitting on what appears to be one of his boxes. If so, all were *not* left behind on the beach. Perhaps the box belongs to one of the other crew members. For comments on the number "42," see note 34.

13. The illustration for this scene deserves careful study. Above deck, left to right, are the Bellman (with a wart on his nose), the Baker (wearing his seven coats and three pairs of boots), and the Barrister. Below deck, left to right: the Billiard-marker, the Banker, the Bonnet-maker (he is making a lady's bonnet), and the Broker.

The Banker's balance scale is for weighing gold, and the loose silver mentioned in Fit 4, stanza 11. Such scales were used in Victorian banks for just this purpose. Everett Bleiler, editor and author, wrote to say that balance scales were also used in English banks for weighing pence instead of counting them.

The Broker is holding his malacca walking cane so that the tip of its imitation amber handle just touches his lips. This was such a common affectation of Victorian fops that canes were commonly called toothpicks. The malacca, made from the dark brown stem of a palm, was usually cloudy or mottled. All of which clarifies the couplet in Canto iv of Pope's *Rape of the Lock*:

He would answer to "Hi!" or to any loud cry,
    Such as "Fry me!" or "Fritter my wig!"[14]
To "What-you-may-call-um!" or "What-was-his-name!"[15]
    But especially "Thing-um-a-jig!"

While, for those who preferred a more forcible word,
    He had different names from these:
His intimate friends called him "Candle-ends,"
    And his enemies "Toasted-cheese."[16]

"His form is ungainly—his intellect small—"
    (So the Bellman would often remark)
"But his courage is perfect! And that, after all,
    Is the thing that one needs with a Snark."

He would joke with hyænas,[17] returning their stare
    With an impudent wag of the head:
And he once went a walk, paw-in-paw, with a bear,
    "Just to keep up its spirits," he said.

Sir Plume, of amber snuff-box vain,
And the nice conduct of a clouded cane.

London dandies with cane handles at their lips can be seen in numerous cartoons of the period (see p. 22, for example), and in the illustrations for many Victorian novels. The practice, with its obvious homosexual symbolism, was not restricted to the malacca. William May Egley's 1859 painting *Omnibus Life in London* (Tate Gallery) shows a pensive, fashionably dressed young man with the handle of a short carrying cane touching his lips.

Correspondent Keith H. Peterson called my attention to the following passage from P. G. Wodehouse's story "Jeeves and the Unbidden Guest":

"Motty, who was sucking the knob of his stick, uncorked himself.
    " 'Yes, mother,' he said, and corked himself up again."

14. Edward B. Jackson of New Zealand wrote to suggest that the Baker's willingness to answer to any loud cry may have been suggested to Carroll by one of Gabriel Oak's dogs, described in chapter 5 of Thomas Hardy's novel *Far from the Madding Crowd*. The book was published two years before the *Snark*.

"So earnest and yet so wrong-headed was this young dog (he had no name in particular, and answered with perfect readiness to any pleasant interjection), that. . . ." The passage goes on to say

The Victorian cane-to-lips gesture.
From *Punch*, 2 July 1870.

that if you sent the dog to chase sheep, it would go on chasing forever unless you stopped it.

"Fry me" and "fritter my wig" are expressions that probably were invented by Carroll; at least I have found no evidence that they were common slang expressions of the time. However, *The Oxford English Dictionary* quotes an old Cornish proverb, "Fry me for a fool and you'll lose your fat in the frying" (citing a reference in *Notes and Queries*, a publication that Carroll read), so it is possible that Carroll had this proverb in mind.

"Fritter my wig" evidently means to mix a wig with batter and fry it in oil or lard to make wig fritters. An alternate meaning: to tear a wig into small pieces. In Carroll's time, sailors referred to shredded sails as "frittered."

15. Joseph Brogunier wrote to me about the significance of "was" in "What-was-his-name."

Both the Baker and the other crew members seem to be anticipating the Baker's vanishing.

16. J. A. Lindon, a British word-puzzle expert, calls my attention to the curious fact that "Candle-ends" (stumps of burned-down candles), "Toasted-cheese," "Fry me," and "Fritter my wig" all refer to objects that are heated. A baker, of course, uses heat in baking, but I incline to the view that the nicknames reflect the crew's awareness that the Baker was perpetually overheated. Although the ship traveled in "tropical climes" (see Fit 2, stanza 7), and note that a hot climate is also suggested by Hope's scanty attire (see illustration on p. 43), the Baker insisted on wearing seven coats and three pairs of boots. This would surely keep him as warm as toasted cheese. Evidently he dreaded the loss of his body heat as much as he dreaded the loss of his existence. The name "Candle-ends" may imply that the Baker is about to burn himself out.

Lindon also points out that both phrases occur in Carroll's long poem *Phantasmagoria*: "candle-ends" in Canto 2, stanza 7, and "toasted cheese" in Canto 3, stanza 13, and Canto 5, stanza 7.

John Clark, in his article "Toasted-Cheese and Candle-Ends" (*Jabberwocky*, Autumn 1985) quotes from a 1594 book about a quack physician who concocts "ointments and sirrups" out of "toasted cheese and candle ends."

Christie Davies, a Welsh sociologist at the University of Reading, sent me an interesting letter in which he argues that "Toasted-cheese" and "Candle-ends" suggest that the Baker was a Welshman from the Cardiganshire county of West Wales. He enclosed several documents to prove that the English once used "toasted-cheese" as a mocking epithet for their Welsh neighbors because toasted cheese (the so-called Welsh rarebit) was a favorite Welsh food. "The English found this dish hilarious," Davies wrote, "much as they laugh at the Scotch for eating porridge or the French for eating frogs and snails."

Why Cardiganshire? Because the "Cardis," who were often tradesmen in the Oxford area,

He came as a Baker: but owned, when too late—
    And it drove the poor Bellman half-mad—
He could only bake Bridecake[18]—for which, I may state,
    No materials were to be had.

The last of the crew needs especial remark,
    Though he looked an incredible dunce:
He had just one idea—but, that one being "Snark,"
    The good Bellman engaged him at once.

He came as a Butcher:[19] but gravely declared,
    When the ship had been sailing a week,
He could only kill Beavers. The Bellman looked scared,
    And was almost too frightened to speak:

But at length he explained, in a tremulous tone,
    There was only one Beaver on board;
And that was a tame one he had of his own,
    Whose death would be deeply deplored.

were regarded by the British as unusually stingy. Indeed, they were defined as "Scotchmen robbed of their generosity." They would naturally, wrote Davies, "devote a ludicrous degree of time and energy to the Gladstonian activity of saving all candle-ends."

17. The species of hyena referred to here is clearly the striped hyena, or laughing hyena, so called because its howl resembles demonic laughter. The Baker later wagged his head at a much more dangerous beast (see Fit 8, stanza 3).

18. Wedding cake.

19. This completes Carroll's description of the ten crew members: Bellman, Boots, Bonnet-maker, Barrister, Broker, Billiard-marker, Banker, Beaver, Baker, and Butcher. To the obvious question of why these names all start with *B*, including also Boojum and Bandersnatch, there are several possible answers. One is suggested in the preface to the Centennial Edition (p. xxvii). Perhaps a better one is suggested by the March Hare at the Mad Tea Party in *Alice's Adventures in Wonderland*. When Alice asked why the three little (Liddell) sisters drew pictures only of objects that begin with *M*, the March Hare replied, "Why not?"

A 1922 letter of Holiday's closes with the following postscript: "I asked Lewis Carroll when first I read his M.S. why he made all the members of the crew have occupations beginning with B. He replied, 'Why not?'"

Carroll used the pseudonym "B.B." in signing some of his early poems. No one knows why, but R. B. Shaberman and Denis Crutch, in their *Under the Quizzing Glass* (London: Magpie Press,

The Beaver, who happened to hear the remark,
   Protested, with tears in its eyes,
That not even the rapture of hunting the Snark
   Could atone for that dismal surprise!

It strongly advised that the Butcher should be
   Conveyed in a separate ship:
But the Bellman declared that would never agree
   With the plans he had made for the trip:

Navigation was always a difficult art,
   Though with only one ship and one bell:
And he feared he must really decline, for his part,
   Undertaking another as well.

The Beaver's best course was, no doubt, to procure
   A second-hand dagger-proof coat—
So the Baker advised it—and next, to insure
   Its life in some Office of note:[20]

1972), make some interesting observations on these initials. In *The Game of Logic* (London: Macmillan, 1887), after having listed such "things" as Buns, Babies, Beetles, Battledores, and their respective attributes, baked, beautiful, black, and broken, Carroll gives (p. 11) the following example of a universal proposition:

"Barzillai Beckalegg is an honest man."

"You think I invented that name, now don't you?" Carroll adds. "But I didn't. It's on a carrier's cart, somewhere down in Cornwall."

Anne Clarke, in her biography of Carroll, defends two other possibilities: Bobby Burns and Beau Brummell.

20. According to *The Oxford English Dictionary* (see entry 8b for "office"), a life insurance company in England, in Carroll's time, was often referred to simply as an "office." "Office of note" means a company of good repute.

This the Banker suggested, and offered for hire[21]
    (On moderate terms), or for sale,
Two excellent Policies, one Against Fire,
    And one Against Damage From Hail.

Yet still, ever after that sorrowful day,
    Whenever the Butcher was by,
The Beaver kept looking the opposite way,[22]
    And appeared unaccountably shy.

21. Hire: rent.

22. In Holiday's illustration for this scene on the ship's bow, note the Butcher's beaver cap. That is not a dagger hanging from his waist; it is a steel for sharpening knives. The Beaver is making lace by the pillow method. A pattern drawn on paper or parchment is placed on the pillow, pins are inserted, and the threads are woven by means of small bobbins.

The Butcher and the Beaver.

Fit the Second

THE BELLMAN'S SPEECH

THE Bellman himself they all praised to the skies—
    Such a carriage, such ease and such grace!
Such solemnity, too! One could see he was wise,
    The moment one looked in his face!

He had bought a large map representing the sea,
    Without the least vestige of land:
And the crew were much pleased when they found it to be
    A map they could all understand.

"What's the good of Mercator's[23] North Poles and Equators,
    Tropics, Zones, and Meridian Lines?"
So the Bellman would cry: and the crew would reply
    "They are merely conventional signs!

"Other maps are such shapes, with their islands and capes!
    But we've got our brave Captain to thank"
(So the crew would protest) "that he's bought us the best—
    A perfect and absolute blank!"[24]

23. Gerhardus Mercator, sixteenth-century Flemish mathematician and cartographer. He devised the method, known as "Mercator's projection," of projecting a spherical map of the earth on a flat rectangle so that the parallels and meridians become straight lines, and the poles become the rectangle's top and bottom edges.

24. In contrast, a map in chapter 11 of Car-

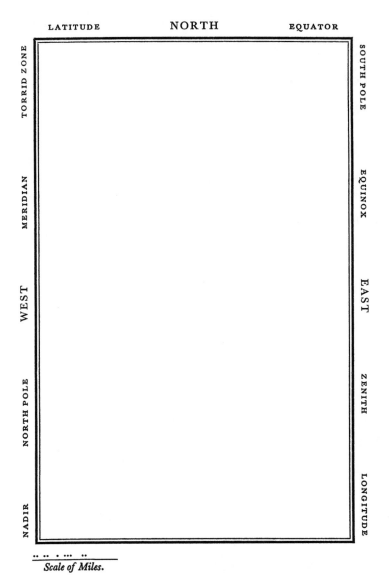

Ocean Chart.

This was charming, no doubt: but they shortly found out
 That the Captain they trusted so well
Had only one notion for crossing the ocean,
 And that was to tingle his bell.[25]

He was thoughtful and grave—but the orders he gave
 Were enough to bewilder a crew.
When he cried, "Steer to starboard, but keep her head larboard!"[26]
 What on earth was the helmsman to do?

Then the bowsprit got mixed with the rudder sometimes:[27]
 A thing, as the Bellman remarked,
That frequently happens in tropical climes,
 When a vessel is, so to speak, "snarked."

roll's *Sylvie and Bruno Concluded*, (volume 2 of *Sylvia and Bruno*, London: Macmillan, 1883) has *everything* on it. The German Professor explains how his country's cartographers experimented with larger and larger maps until they finally made one with a scale of a mile to the mile. "It has never been spread out, yet," he says. "The farmers objected: they said it would cover the whole country, and shut out the sunlight! So now we use the country itself, as its own map, and I assure you it does nearly as well."

25. This use of the word *tingle* was common enough in the eighteenth century but already rare in Carroll's day. Perhaps, as correspondent James T. de Kay has observed, Carroll chose this word to evoke subtly the spine-tingling terror that will soon overtake the crew.

Edward Guiliano, in a talk on the *Snark* published in *Lewis Carroll: A Celebration*, stressed the roll of the Bellman's bell in constantly reminding the reader of the inescapable passage of time as the crew moves toward its destiny. Bells were used on ships and in schools, as well as by town criers, to mark time, and they are tolled by churches to indicate death. The bell is in every illustration of the original book except the blank map on which time is meaningless. Holiday's rendering of the Bellman, Guiliano notes, suggests a wise father-time figure.

"This poem," Guiliano concluded his talk, "which on the literal level has so many humorous moments, turns out to be the saddest of Carroll's writing. The ending is not at all funny. One character vanishes, and another, the Bellman, remains a grave and depressing figure. He has, after all, but one notion of navigation, and that is to tingle his bell."

26. *Larboard* is another name for *port*. The instructions are, of course, contradictory.

27. The bowsprit can be seen clearly in two of Holiday's illustrations. In his preface Carroll explains exactly why the bowsprit occasionally got mixed with the rudder. This confusion is often cited by Freudian critics of Carroll,

But the principal failing occurred in the sailing,
    And the Bellman, perplexed and distressed,
Said he *had* hoped, at least, when the wind blew due East,
    That the ship would *not* travel due West!

But the danger was past—they had landed at last,
    With their boxes, portmanteaus, and bags:
Yet at first sight the crew were not pleased with the view,
    Which consisted of chasms and crags.

The Bellman perceived that their spirits were low,
    And repeated in musical tone
Some jokes he had kept for a season of woe—
    But the crew would do nothing but groan.

He served out some grog with a liberal hand,
    And bade them sit down on the beach:
And they could not but own that their Captain looked grand,
    As he stood and delivered his speech.

"Friends, Romans, and countrymen, lend me your ears!"[28]
    (They were all of them fond of quotations:
So they drank to his health, and they gave him three cheers,
    While he served out additional rations).

though they are a bit vague as to just what to make of it.

The confusion of bowsprit and rudder may also be a way of saying that the ship occasionally sailed backward, as Carroll's preface tells us it did. Denis Crutch has pointed out (*Jabberwocky*, Autumn 1976) that the Bellman's order, in the previous stanza, to steer to starboard but keep the ship's head to port, is a maneuver that could be executed only by going backward and in a circle.

It would explain, Crutch says, why half the time the ship went west when the wind blew due east. "It is my belief," he concludes, "that they merely circumnavigated their own island, ending near where they began."

28. Surely no reader will fail to recognize this opening line (with an added "and") of Mark Antony's oration at Caesar's funeral, in Shakespeare's *Julius Caesar*.

"We have sailed many months, we have sailed many weeks,
    (Four weeks to the month you may mark),
But never as yet ('tis your Captain who speaks)
    Have we caught the least glimpse of a Snark!

"We have sailed many weeks, we have sailed many days,
    (Seven days to the week I allow),
But a Snark, on the which we might lovingly gaze,
    We have never beheld till now!

"Come, listen, my men, while I tell you again
    The five unmistakable marks
By which you may know, wheresoever you go,
    The warranted genuine Snarks.

"Let us take them in order. The first is the taste,
    Which is meagre and hollow, but crisp:
Like a coat that is rather too tight in the waist,
    With a flavour of Will-o-the-wisp.

"Its habit of getting up late you'll agree
    That it carries too far, when I say
That it frequently breakfasts at five-o'clock tea,
    And dines on the following day.

"The third is its slowness in taking a jest.
    Should you happen to venture on one,
It will sigh like a thing that is deeply distressed:
    And it always looks grave at a pun.

"The fourth is its fondness for bathing-machines,[29]
    Which it constantly carries about,
And believes that they add to the beauty of scenes—
    A sentiment open to doubt.

"The fifth is ambition. It next will be right
    To describe each particular batch:
Distinguishing those that have feathers, and bite,
    From those that have whiskers, and scratch.

"For, although common Snarks do no manner of harm,
    Yet, I feel it my duty to say,
Some are Boojums—"[30] The Bellman broke off in alarm,
    For the Baker had fainted away.

29. Bathing-machines were individual wooden locker rooms on wheels. While the modest Victorian bather changed into bathing clothes, horses (surrounded by flies) would pull the machine into several feet of water. The bather would then emerge through a door facing the sea, screened by a large awning attached to the machine. At many beaches a guide, or "dipper," would forcibly assist the reluctant bather to make the icy plunge.

In one of Carroll's playful letters to Gertrude Chataway he proposes visiting her at Sandown, the summer resort where they first met. If she is unable to find a room for him, he expects her to give him *her* room and to spend the night by herself on the beach. "If you . . . feel a little chilly, of course you could go into a bathing machine, which everybody knows is *very* comfortable to sleep in—you know they make the floor of soft wood on purpose. I send you seven kisses (to last a week). . . ."

There are many references to bathing-machines in Victorian literature. The Lord Chancellor, in the Gilbert and Sullivan operetta *Iolanthe*, sings about "lying awake with a dismal headache" and dreaming of crossing the channel in rough weather on a steamer from Harwich that is "something between a large bathing machine and a very small second-class carriage."

The following ode to the bathing-machine appeared anonymously in *Punch*, 1 September 1883:

BEHOLD an old relic of old-fashioned days,
    Recalling the coaches, the hoy, and
      postchaise!
It has not advanced in a timber or wheel,
    Since first it was fashioned by Benjamin
      Beale.

It is not æsthetic, nor yet picturesque,
    'Tis heavy and cumbrous, expensive,
      grotesque—
And I feel very certain there never was seen
    Such an old-fashioned thing as a
      Bathing Machine!

Bathing-machines. From *Punch*, 9 September 1876.

The windows won't open, the doors never fit,
  The floor is strewn over with pebbles
    and grit;
A looking-glass too, with a silverless back,
  A pinless pincushion, a broken boot-jack:

It smells of old seaweed, 'tis mouldy and grim,
  'Tis sloppy and stuffy, 'tis dismal and dim—
'Tis a deer-cart, a fish-van, or something
    between;
  Oh, a hideous hutch is the Bathing Machine!

The driver says "Right!" and he raps at the door;
  He starts with a jerk, and you sit on the floor!
It creaks and it rattles, you rise and you fall,
  And bound to and fro like a mad tennis-ball!

Again there's a lurch, and you nearly fall flat,
  And first sprain your ankle, then tread on
    your hat—
While you're bumped and you're battered,
    bruised blue, black, and green,
  In that horrid contrivance, the Bathing
    Machine!

For more on bathing-machines, see chapter 2, note 7, of *Alice's Adventures in Wonderland,* in *The Annotated Alice* (New York: W. W. Norton, 2000), and *The English Seaside* by H. G. Stokes (London: Sylvan Press, 1947), pp. 17–25. The pages of *Punch* contain scores of cartoons about bathing-machines, including the variety that dotted the French coast (for example, see p. 33).

30. In chapter 24 of *Sylvie and Bruno Concluded,* the second half of Carroll's long, sentimental fantasy novel (the first half was published thirteen years after the *Snark*), the following dialogue occurs:

> "The Professor sighed, and gave it up. 'Do you know what a Boojum is?'
>
> "'*I* know!' cried Bruno. 'It's the thing what wrenches people out of their boots!'
>
> "'He means "bootjack,"' Sylvie explained in a whisper.

"'You can't wrench people out of *boots,*' the Professor mildly observed.

"Bruno laughed saucily. 'Oo *can,* though! Unless they're *welly* tight in.'

"'Once upon a time there was a Boojum—' the Professor began, but stopped suddenly. 'I forget the rest of the Fable,' he said. 'And there was a lesson to be learned from it. I'm afraid I forget *that,* too.'"

Various attempts have been made to explain the word *Boojum.* Linguistic expert Eric Partridge in his essay "The Nonsense Words of Edward Lear and Lewis Carroll" (in his book *Here, There and Everywhere,* London: Hamish Hamilton, 1950) suggests that it packs together *Boo!* and *fee, fo, fi, fum!* Phyllis Greenacre points out that in addition to suggesting *Boo!* it also suggests *boohoo.* One thinks also of *boogieman,* though in Carroll's England it was pronounced with a long *o* and spelled *bogy* or *bogey.* The Old Bogy was the Devil, and a bogy was an evil goblin or anything that aroused terror. The Bogyman was supposed to "get" little children if they misbehaved.

Thanks to the tireless efforts of physicist N. David Mermin, the word *Boojum* has now entered the language of physics. It is a singularity that can form in superfluid helium-3, and that works its way to the surface where it can make a supercurrent softly and suddenly vanish. See Mermin's "E. Pluribus Boojum" in *Physics Today* (April 1981) and *Boojums All the Way Through* (Cambridge: Cambridge University Press, 1990). See also "Let Us Now Praise Famous Boojums" by M. Mitchell Waldrop in *Science,* vol. 212, 19 June 1981, page 1378.

A few years earlier the word *snark* was adopted in graph theory as the name for a certain rare species of graphs that have three lines meeting at each point. See my book *The Last Recreations* (New York: Copernicos, 1997), chapter 23, and the section on snarks in *Edge-Colourings of Graphs,* by S. Fiorini and R. J. Wilson (London: Pitman, 1977), pp. 47–50.

J. A. Lindon notes that *Boojum* is a syllable reversal of *Jumbo*, the name P. T. Barnum gave to a huge elephant that he bought in 1882 from the London Zoo. The word came to be applied to other elephants and to any oversize object. Lindon also observed that the elephant is one of those huge beasts for which one can confuse rudder and bowsprit.

Note also that *boojum* is inside *mumbo jumbo*, a synonym for gibberish. The phrase derives from what was said to be the name of an African idol.

Boojum is now a common vernacular name for a slithy, queer-shaped tree that thrives only in the central desert of Mexico's Baja California. Joseph Wood Krutch, in his book *The Forgotten Peninsula* (New York: W. Sloan, 1961), devotes an entire chapter to the Boojum. What does it look like? Answers Krutch: like nothing else on earth. Natives call it a *cirio* (wax candle) because it resembles a candle, though its body is covered with what from a distance seems to be a rough hairy growth but on closer inspection proves to be a stubble of short twigs. "Perhaps only a botanist could love it," writes Krutch. Fully grown specimens reach a height of fifty feet, sometimes drooping over in an arch until the tip touches the ground. Standing in a forest of Boojums, Krutch found the effect hallucinatory, like a surrealist dream.

The name *Boojum* was given to the tree by the British ecologist Godfrey Sykes when he explored the Baja in 1922. Like Carroll's Banker, Sykes carried with him a telescope. According to his son's account, he focused his telescope on a distant tree, gazed intently for a few moments, then said, "Ho, ho, a boojum, definitely a boojum."

Any readers who wish to learn more about this absurd tree can consult an entire book on it that was published in 1971 by the University of Arizona Press: *The Boojum and Its Home*, by Robert R. Humphrey. And if readers are near Phoenix, Arizona, they will find specimens of Boojums in the botanical gardens there.

Fit the Third

THE BAKER'S TALE

THEY roused him with muffins—they roused him with ice—
　　They roused him with mustard and cress—[31]
They roused him with jam and judicious advice—
　　They set him conundrums to guess.

When at length he sat up and was able to speak,
　　His sad story he offered to tell;
And the Bellman cried "Silence! Not even a shriek!"
　　And excitedly tingled his bell.

There was silence supreme! Not a shriek, not a scream,
　　Scarcely even a howl or a groan,
As the man they called "Ho!" told his story of woe
　　In an antediluvian tone.[32]

31. Mustard and cress, a common salad and sandwich ingredient in England, is grown from a mixture of the seeds of white mustard and garden cress. When the shoots are about an inch tall, they are cut with scissors and placed between thin slices of bread to make sandwiches for four o'clock tea.

32. Eric Partridge (*Here, There, and Everywhere*) calls attention to this line as one of those rare instances in which Carroll uses a standard word in a completely whimsical sense. Such words occur often in Lear's verse (e.g., "That intrinsic old man of Peru," "He weareth a runcible hat," "Sweetly susceptible blue," "Propitious old man with a beard").

Several correspondents have disagreed with Partridge. They suggest that "antediluvian" may foreshadow the Baker's tears two stanzas later.

"My father and mother were honest, though poor—"[33]
  "Skip all that!" cried the Bellman in haste.
"If it once becomes dark, there's no chance of a Snark—
  We have hardly a minute to waste!"

"I skip forty years,"[34] said the Baker, in tears,
  "And proceed without further remark
To the day when you took me aboard of your ship
  To help you in hunting the Snark.

"A dear uncle of mine (after whom I was named)
  Remarked, when I bade him farewell—"
"Oh, skip your dear uncle!" the Bellman exclaimed,
  As he angrily tingled his bell.

33. A sly reversal of a common phrase, "born to poor but honest parents . . . ," that begins so many early novels and autobiographies.

34. The skipping of forty years puts the Baker in his early forties. Carroll began writing the *Snark* in 1874 when he was 42. Could the Baker be Carroll himself? J. A. Lindon suggests that the Baker's 42 boxes (Fit 1, stanza 7) are perhaps intended to represent Carroll's 42 years. Each box bore the Baker's name, and all were left behind when he joined the Snark-hunting expedition. Note also the mention of Rule 42 in Carroll's preface, and the King's remarks at the trial of the Knave of Hearts (*Alice's Adventures in Wonderland*, chapter 12): "Rule Forty-two. *All persons more than a mile high to leave the court.*" Curiously, Carroll refers to his age as 42 in his poem *Phantasmagoria* (Canto 1, stanza 16), though at the time this poem was written he was still in his thirties. The number 42 certainly seems to have had some sort of special significance for Carroll.

J. A. Lindon has noticed that if we take the memorable date of 4 July 1862 (on which Carroll began telling Alice Liddell the story of *Alice in Wonderland*) and write it, British style, as 4/7/62, we have a number with 76 in the middle (the publication year of the *Snark*) and 42 on the ends. R. B. Shaberman and Denis Crutch, in *Under the Quizzing Glass*, point out that the first Alice book has just 42 illustrations, and the second book would have had the same number had it not been for a last-minute change of plan.

Lindon also recalls that the number of horses and men sent to repair Humpty Dumpty is 4,207. Alice's age in the second Alice book is 7 years and 6 months, and 6 times 7, Lindon observes, is 42. Indeed, the number 42 calls to mind the common phrase "all sixes and sevens," but one could go on for pages with this kind of number juggling.

Other passages strengthen the view that Carroll was satirizing himself in the person of the Baker. The Baker's ungainly form and small intellect, his absentmindedness, his pseudonyms, his tidy packing of boxes, his ways of joking with hyenas and walking with bears, his waggishness,

"He remarked to me then," said that mildest of men,
"'If your Snark be a Snark, that is right:
Fetch it home by all means—you may serve it with greens,
And it's handy for striking a light.[35]

"'You may seek it with thimbles—and seek it with care;
You may hunt it with forks and hope;
You may threaten its life with a railway-share;
You may charm it with smiles and soap—'"

("That's exactly the method," the Bellman bold
In a hasty parenthesis cried,
"That's exactly the way I have always been told
That the capture of Snarks should be tried!")

"'But oh, beamish[36] nephew, beware of the day,
If your Snark be a Boojum! For then
You will softly and suddenly vanish away,
And never be met with again!'

---

his wakeful nights, his vanishing in the midst of laughter and glee—all add up to a whimsical, funny-sad, self-deprecating portrait.

In my new preface to this edition I mention a clear indication, which inexplicably I had not realized before, that Carroll intended the Baker to be a caricature of himself. In stanza 6 of this fit the Baker speaks of "A dear uncle of mine (after whom I was named)." Carroll's uncle was Robert Wilfred Skeffington Lutwidge, and Charles Dodgson's middle name was Lutwidge!

35. Carroll may have intended this to suggest that the Snark breathes out fire like a dragon, or possibly that the beast's hide is a rough surface on which matches can be struck.

36. This is the first use in the *Snark* of a nonsense word from "Jabberwock." The word is not exactly nonsense: *The Oxford English Dictionary* traces it back to 1530 as a variant of *beaming*.

"It is this, it is this that oppresses my soul,
    When I think of my uncle's last words:[37]
And my heart is like nothing so much as a bowl
    Brimming over with quivering curds!

"It is this, it is this—" "We have had that before!"
    The Bellman indignantly said.
And the Baker replied "Let me say it once more.
    It is this, it is this that I dread!

"I engage with the Snark—every night after dark—
    In a dreamy delirious fight:
I serve it with greens in those shadowy scenes,
    And I use it for striking a light:

"But if ever I meet with a Boojum, that day,
    In a moment (of this I am sure),
I shall softly and suddenly vanish away—
    And the notion I cannot endure!"

37. Apparently Holiday interpreted "last words" to mean that the Baker's uncle died after speaking them. At any rate, he pictures the uncle as confined to bed, hands crippled by arthritis, his medicine on a shelf above.

The Baker's Tale.

Fit the Fourth

THE HUNTING

THE Bellman looked uffish,[38] and wrinkled his brow.
     "If only you'd spoken before!
It's excessively awkward to mention it now,
     With the Snark, so to speak, at the door!

"We should all of us grieve, as you well may believe,
     If you never were met with again—
But surely, my man, when the voyage began,
     You might have suggested it then?

"It's excessively awkward to mention it now—
     As I think I've already remarked."
And the man they called "Hi!" replied, with a sigh,
     "I informed you the day we embarked.

"You may charge me with murder—or want of sense—
     (We are all of us weak at times):
But the slightest approach to a false pretence
     Was never among my crimes!

"I said it in Hebrew—I said it in Dutch—
    I said it in German and Greek:
But I wholly forgot (and it vexes me much)
    That English is what you speak!"

"'Tis a pitiful tale," said the Bellman, whose face
    Had grown longer at every word:
"But, now that you've stated the whole of your case,
    More debate would be simply absurd.

"The rest of my speech" (he explained to his men)
    "You shall hear when I've leisure to speak it.
But the Snark is at hand, let me tell you again!
    'Tis your glorious duty to seek it!

"To seek it with thimbles, to seek it with care;
    To pursue it with forks and hope;
To threaten its life with a railway-share;
    To charm it with smiles and soap!

"For the Snark's a peculiar creature, that won't
    Be caught in a commonplace way.
Do all that you know, and try all that you don't:
    Not a chance must be wasted to-day!

"For England expects—I forbear to proceed:
    'Tis a maxim tremendous, but trite:[39]
And you'd best be unpacking the things that you need
    To rig yourselves out for the fight."

39. The tremendous but trite maxim is, of course, "England expects every man to do his duty." It was a flag signal to the fleet, ordered by Horatio Nelson shortly before he was killed by a musket shot at the battle of Trafalgar in 1805. According to one account of the episode, Nelson

The Hunting.

Then the Banker endorsed a blank cheque (which he crossed),[40]
And changed his loose silver for notes.
The Baker with care combed his whiskers and hair,[41]
And shook the dust out of his coats.

The Boots and the Broker were sharpening a spade——[42]
Each working the grindstone in turn:
But the Beaver went on making lace, and displayed
No interest in the concern:

Though the Barrister tried to appeal to its pride,
And vainly proceeded to cite
A number of cases, in which making laces
Had been proved an infringement of right.

The maker of Bonnets ferociously planned
A novel arrangement of bows:
While the Billiard-marker with quivering hand
Was chalking the tip of his nose.

first ordered the signal "Nelson confides that every man will do his duty." An officer suggested replacing *Nelson* with *England*, and it was pointed out that *expects* was in the flag code whereas *confides* would have to be spelled out with a flag for each letter. (For details, see the Oxford journal *Notes and Queries*, ser. 6, vol. 9, pp. 261 and 283.)

"If . . . England expects every man to do his duty," Dickens wrote in *Martin Chuzzlewit*, chapter 43, "England is the most sanguine country on the face of the earth, and will find itself continually disappointed."

40. The practice of crossing checks is still standard throughout the United Kingdom, and is one of the principal ways in which the English system of checking differs from that of the United States. To cross a check "generally," the

writer draws two slanting and parallel lines across the face and writes "& Co." between them. This means that the check is not negotiable; it must be deposited to the payee's bank account. To cross a check "specially," the name of the bank where the amount is to be deposited is written across the face of the check. English banks now issue ready-crossed checks, with the parallel lines printed on them, and many people carry checks of both crossed and uncrossed varieties.

41. The Baker appears whiskerless in Holiday's illustrations. Either Holiday failed to note that the Baker combed his whiskers, or Carroll added this stanza after it was too late to alter the art, or there is a small, almost invisible tuft of side whiskers below the Baker's left ear in the illustration that shows him sitting on the deck.

But the Butcher turned nervous, and dressed himself fine,
 With yellow kid gloves and a ruff—
Said he felt it exactly like going to dine,
 Which the Bellman declared was all "stuff."[43]

"Introduce me, now there's a good fellow," he said,
 "If we happen to meet it together!"
And the Bellman, sagaciously nodding his head,
 Said "That must depend on the weather."

The Beaver went simply galumphing[44] about,
 At seeing the Butcher so shy:
And even the Baker, though stupid and stout,
 Made an effort to wink with one eye.

"Be a man!" said the Bellman in wrath, as he heard
 The Butcher beginning to sob.
"Should we meet with a Jubjub,[45] that desperate bird,
 We shall need all our strength for the job!"

42. Why in the world, Everett Bleiler wonders, were they sharpening a spade?

43. *Stuff*, a slang equivalent of *rubbish* or *stuff and nonsense*, was current in Carroll's day. However, as correspondent Thomas Wray pointed out, the primary meaning of *stuff* is a cloth, usually woolen, and often opposed to fine clothes made of silk or linen. "An example of this opposition," he writes, "is found in British legal robes. Silk is used for the gowns of legal barristers, junior barristers wearing stuff gowns. . . . Is not the Bellman disparaging the Butcher's finery by declaring it to be mere stuff?"

44. *Galumphing*, from "Jabberwocky," is one of Carroll's portmanteau words that have entered the dictionary. It is a blend of *gallop* and triumphant, meaning (according to *The Oxford English Dictionary*) "to march on exultantly with irregular bounding movements." "Both Carroll and Lear," writes Eric Partridge, "must, in their philological heaven, be chortling at the thought that they have frabjously galumphed their way into the English vocabulary" (*Here, There and Everywhere*).

45. "Beware the Jubjub bird" reads a line in the second stanza of "Jabberwocky." Eric Partridge thinks *Jubjub* may be a pun on *jug-jug*, an English word expressing one of the notes of the nightingale; perhaps a blend of *jug-jug* and *hubbub* (*Here, There and Everywhere*).

Fit the Fifth

THE BEAVER'S LESSON

THEY sought it with thimbles, they sought it with care;
 They pursued it with forks and hope,[46]
They threatened its life with a railway-share;
 They charmed it with smiles and soap.[47]

Then the Butcher contrived an ingenious plan
 For making a separate sally;
And had fixed on a spot unfrequented by man,
 A dismal and desolate valley.

46. Elspeth Huxley gave the title *With Forks and Hope* to her African notebook, published in the United States by Morrow in 1964.

47. This is the third appearance of this stanza but the first to describe the actual carrying out of the Snark-hunting method advised by the Baker's uncle. (For translations of the stanza into French, Latin, Dutch, Swedish, Danish, German, and Italian, see the bibliography.) The fact that essentially the same stanza occurs altogether six times in the poem has led some to suspect that it may conceal a private, cryptic message. If so, the message has never been decoded.

My theory—the reader may be able to formulate a better one—is that thimbles, forks, a railway share, smiles, and soap are connected with the Snark's five unmistakable marks mentioned in Fit 2. The forks are for eating crisp Snark meat. The railway share appeals to the Snark's ambition to become wealthy and so can be used for baiting a death trap. Smiles are to let the Snark know when a pun has been perpetrated. The soap is of course for the bathing-machines that the Snark carries about, and the thimble is used for thumping the side of the creature's head to wake him in time for five-o'clock tea.

The bare-bosomed young woman in Holiday's illustration for this stanza is Hope. (She may also be the ship's wooden figurehead. See the illustration on p. 43.) It is amusing to note that when Scotish writer and critic Andrew Lang reviewed the *Snark* in 1876 he failed completely to identify

But the very same plan to the Beaver occurred:
　　It had chosen the very same place:
Yet neither betrayed, by a sign or a word,
　　The disgust that appeared in his face.

Each thought he was thinking of nothing but "Snark"
　　And the glorious work of the day;
And each tried to pretend that he did not remark[48]
　　That the other was going that way.

But the valley grew narrow and narrower still,
　　And the evening got darker and colder,
Till (merely from nervousness, not from goodwill)
　　They marched along shoulder to shoulder.

the young lady. "In a sketch of the whole crew," he wrote, "there is a really graceful half-draped female figure with an anchor and a trident, who may or may not be the Bonnet-maker, but who would deeply shock the Banker at her side."

It is not by accident that Holiday placed a sheet anchor on Hope's shoulder. As far back as the sixteenth century, the term *sheet anchor* has been figuratively used for that on which one ultimately relies: one's mainstay, after all else has failed. Artists in England traditionally depicted Hope with such an anchor.

Joseph Keogh, a Canadian correspondent, called attention to the draped figure of Britania, a symbol of Great Britain who appeared on the old English copper pennies. She is there shown holding a trident like the one held by Hope. The trident was traditionally carried by the Roman sea god Neptune.

The woman with bowed head is Care. (She is also mentioned in the opening stanza of the poem; the Bellman lands her with the crew.) There are five "forks" in the picture if we count

Hope's anchor as a fork. In the upper left corner are the Broker, still sucking his cane, and the Baker. The Barrister is wearing his wig and legal robes. The Banker carries a tuning fork (appropriate, as J. A. Lindon suggests in a letter to me, to a man who deals in notes) and the telescope that he is seen holding in the ballad's first illustration. The Beaver holds a microscope.

Carroll does not mention either the microscope or telescope. Perhaps the Beaver is searching for microscopic clues, such as a bit of feather or whisker, and the Banker hopes to spot a Snark in the far distance. The instruments are also appropriate, as Lindon has observed, to the habits of the two crew members: a Banker must constantly be looking ahead on his investments, whereas a Beaver is concerned only with what is directly under its nose. (Cf. the railway scene in chapter 3 of *Through the Looking-Glass*, in which the Guard looks at Alice first through a telescope, then through a microscope.)

48. *Remark* in the sense of *observe* or *notice*, not in the sense of making a remark.

Then a scream, shrill and high, rent the shuddering sky,
 And they knew that some danger was near:
The Beaver turned pale to the tip of its tail,
 And even the Butcher felt queer.

He thought of his childhood, left far far behind—
 That blissful and innocent state—
The sound so exactly recalled to his mind
 A pencil that squeaks on a slate!

" 'Tis the voice of the Jubjub!"[49] he suddenly cried.
 (This man, that they used to call "Dunce.")
"As the Bellman would tell you," he added with pride,
 "I have uttered that sentiment once.

" 'Tis the note of the Jubjub! Keep count, I entreat;
 You will find I have told it you twice.
'Tis the song of the Jubjub! The proof is complete,
 If only I've stated it thrice."[50]

49. Cf. " 'Tis the voice of the Lobster" (*Alice's Adventures in Wonderland*, chapter 10), Carroll's parody on the opening lines of Isaac Watts's poem "The Sluggard" (" 'Tis the voice of the sluggard"). All three lines derive ultimately from the biblical phrase (Song of Songs 2:12) "the voice of the turtle."

Note the similarity between *Jubjub* and *bulbul*, a Persian songbird often mentioned in Victorian poetry.

50. Joseph Brogunier called my attention to the importance of "if" in this line. The Butcher is not certain that he has made a statement three times; indeed, there are good grounds for his and the Beaver's doubts. When the Bellman invoked the rule-of-three at the beginning of Fit 1, he had thrice repeated exactly the same words, "Just the place for a Snark." But the Butcher refers first to the Jubjub's voice, then to its note, and finally to its song. Later, when he tries to prove that he *did* repeat himself thrice, he invokes an irrelevant mathematical argument that begs the question.

Is not all this a striking allegory of American philosopher Charles Peirce's obsessive preoccupation with monads, dyads, and triads? The Butcher's "queer" feeling (a "queer being" was how William James once described his friend Peirce), when he hears the Jubjub's first scream, is surely an experience of Firstness. But as soon as he recalls the sound's resemblance to a sound heard in childhood, it becomes an experience of Second-

The Beaver had counted with scrupulous care,
   Attending to every word:
But it fairly lost heart, and outgrabe[51] in despair,
   When the third repetition occurred.

It felt that, in spite of all possible pains,
   It had somehow contrived to lose count,
And the only thing now was to rack its poor brains
   By reckoning up the amount.

"Two added to one—if that could but be done,"
   It said, "with one's fingers and thumbs!"
Recollecting with tears how, in earlier years,
   It had taken no pains with its sums.

"The thing can be done," said the Butcher, "I think.
   The thing must be done, I am sure.
The thing shall be done! Bring me paper and ink,
   The best there is time to procure."

ness. And when he recognizes the sound as a song, exhibiting continuity in time, he experiences Thirdness.

Can the validity of the three categories be proved? After expressing his beliefs in a triad of modalities (the proof can, must, and shall be done), the Butcher requests paper and ink on which he can write equations and draw existential graphs to show that if you start with Thirdness you can't go any higher. You just keep producing more triads. Note that the Butcher writes with a "pen in each hand" (stanza 15). Although Peirce was left-handed, we are told by Paul Weiss (in his article on Peirce in *The Dictionary of American Biography*) that Peirce could "write with both hands—in fact, he was capable of writing a ques-

tion with one hand and the answer simultaneously with the other."

Peirce, like the Butcher, was convinced that his three categories of Firstness, Secondness, and Thirdness were "exactly and perfectly true." They revealed to him what had previously been "enveloped in absolute mystery," and he would gladly explain his method, in his famous "popular style," if only he had the time, and if his listeners had the brains to understand. There is so much that "remains to be said"! (No book on philosophy was published by Peirce in his lifetime, but he had endless projects for monumental works that he hoped to write.)

Observe the significant reference in stanza 8 to the Butcher having been called "Dunce." This

The Beaver brought paper, portfolio, pens,[52]
And ink in unfailing supplies:
While strange creepy creatures came out of their dens,
And watched them with wondering eyes.

So engrossed was the Butcher, he heeded them not,
As he wrote with a pen in each hand,
And explained all the while in a popular style
Which the Beaver could well understand.

unquestionably is a reference to Duns Scotus, the medieval philosopher Peirce most admired, and whose realism had such a strong influence on Peirce's phenomenology.

The Beaver, in my allegory, is none other than philosopher Charles Hartshorne, coeditor with Weiss of Peirce's *Collected Papers* and the most distinguished living defender of Peirce's three categories. From Peirce's "Lesson" he learns more in ten minutes than he could learn in a lifetime of reading. Although Hartshorne is destined to have many quarrels with Peirce, he need only remember his great encounter with the Jubjub's Firstness, Secondness, and Thirdness to have his admiration and affection for Peirce restored.

"I believe," wrote Hartshorne, "that all things, from atoms to God, are really instances of First, Second, Third, and that no other equally simple doctrine has the power and precision of this one, when purified of its synechistic excesses." See Hartshorne's paper "Charles Peirce's 'One Contribution to Philosophy' and His Most Serious Mistake," in *Studies in the Philosophy of Charles Sanders Peirce*, 2d ser., edited by E. C. Moore and R. S. Robin (Amherst: University of Massachusetts Press, 1964).

My references to Peirce, Duns Scotus, and Hartshorne are of course intended as jokes. I doubt if Carroll had ever heard of Peirce, and Hartshorne was born after Carroll died.

51. *Outgrabe* is from the first stanza of "Jabberwocky." Humpty Dumpty explains that *outgribing* "is something between bellowing and whistling, with a kind of sneeze in the middle: however, you'll hear it done, maybe—down in the wood yonder—and, when you've once heard it, you'll be *quite* content."

52. J. A. Lindon suggests in a personal letter that the illustration for this scene may have been intended as one of those puzzle pictures in which you try to spot as many objects as you can that begin with a certain letter, in this case the letter *B*. The list includes: Butcher, Beaver, Bellman, bell, barrel organs, bats, bugles, band, bottles, books, brace, and bit. In Holiday's original sketch there is a book beneath Colenso's that is titled *Bridge*.

Correspondent Eric Hyman, taking his cue from the fact that the Beaver brought along "paper, portfolio, pens," wrote to defend the letter *P*. Other *P* words include plumes, pigs, pussy cats, points, pocket, piccolo, and pipes.

The picture has many fascinating details. Note the lizard labeled "income tax" that is rifling the Butcher's pockets. The kittens are playing with the Butcher's yellow kid gloves. The large object in the lower right corner is an ornate inkstand called a "standish."

Colenso's *Arithmetic*, at the Butcher's feet, was a popular schoolbook of the day. (A copy was

The Beaver's Lesson.

"Taking Three as the subject to reason about—
A convenient number to state—
We add Seven, and Ten, and then multiply out
By One Thousand diminished by Eight.

"The result we proceed to divide, as you see,
By Nine Hundred and Ninety and Two:
Then subtract Seventeen, and the answer must be
Exactly and perfectly true.[53]

listed among Carroll's books that were auctioned after his death.) It was written by Bishop (note the *B*!) John William Colenso, one of the great controversial figures of the Victorian era. He began his career as a mathematical tutor and author of a series of mathematics textbooks widely used throughout England. In 1846 he was appointed Bishop of Natal, a South African province where the native Zulus badgered him with embarrassing questions about the Old Testament. The more Colenso pondered his answers the more he convinced himself that Christianity was lost if it continued to insist on the Bible's historical accuracy. He expressed these heretical views in a series of books, using arithmetical arguments to prove the nonsense of various Old Testament tales. How, for example, could 12,000 Israelites slaughter 200,000 Midianites? This atrocity, the bishop decided, "had happily only been carried out on paper." Such opinions seem mild today, but at the time they touched off a tempest that rocked the English church. Colenso was savagely denounced, socially ostracized, and finally excommunicated, though the courts decided in his favor and he was later reinstated at Natal.

It is appropriate that the second book in Holiday's illustration is *On the Reductio ad Absurdum*. Just as Carroll reduced the sea ballad to absurdity, so Colenso reduced to absurdity the literal interpretation of the Bible. Was Carroll pro or con Colenso? I have been unable to find out. He surely would have sided with the bishop in his attacks on the doctrine of eternal punishment, but it is doubtful if he would have favored Colenso's defence of polygamy among Zulu converts or the degree to which the bishop dismissed biblical stories as mythology.

For an interesting article on Colenso, see "The Colenso Controversy" by P. O. G. White in *Theology*, vol. 65, October 1962, pp. 402–8.

The winged pigs derive from the old Scottish proverb "Pigs may fly, but it's not likely." "Just about as much right as pigs have to fly," says the Duchess in *Alice's Adventures in Wonderland* (chapter 9), and in *Through the Looking-Glass* (chapter 4) Tweedledee sings:

And why the sea is boiling hot—
And whether pigs have wings.

53. It is good to have clearly in mind what is going on here. The Butcher is fairly certain that he has made his statement three times; according to the Bellman's rule-of-three, this proves the truth of his assertion. The Beaver counted the first two statements, but had difficulty adding them to the last one. The Butcher is proving to the Beaver that 2 plus 1 does in fact equal 3. His arithmetical procedure is a sterling example of circular reasoning. It begins with 3, the number

"The method employed I would gladly explain,
  While I have it so clear in my head,
If I had but the time and you had but the brain—
  But much yet remains to be said.

"In one moment I've seen what has hitherto been
  Enveloped in absolute mystery,
And without extra charge I will give you at large
  A Lesson in Natural History."[54]

he seeks to prove, and ends with 3; but the procedure is such that he is certain to end with whatever number he starts with. If x be the starting number, the procedure can be expressed algebraically as:

$$\frac{(x + 7 + 10)(1000-8)}{992} -17$$

which simplifies to x.

54. Phyllis Greenacre thinks that the ten members of the crew represent the ten children in the Dodgson family, with Charles as the Baker. "The part of the poem in which the Butcher gives the docile Beaver a lesson in natural history," she writes, "is probably [analysts often have difficulty writing "possibly"] but a thinly disguised picture of a consultation among the little Dodgsons regarding the mysterious [sex] life of their awesome parents" (*Swift and Carroll*).

In his genial way he proceeded to say
    (Forgetting all laws of propriety,
And that giving instruction, without introduction,
    Would have caused quite a thrill in Society),

"As to temper the Jubjub's a desperate bird,
    Since it lives in perpetual passion:
Its taste in costume is entirely absurd—
    It is ages ahead of the fashion:

"But it knows any friend it has met once before:
    It never will look at a bribe:
And in charity-meetings it stands at the door,
    And collects—though it does not subscribe.

"Its flavour when cooked is more exquisite far
    Than mutton, or oysters, or eggs:
(Some think it keeps best in an ivory jar,
    And some, in mahogany kegs:)

"You boil it in sawdust: you salt it in glue:
    You condense it with locusts and tape:
Still keeping one principal object in view—
    To preserve its symmetrical shape."[55]

55. The late H. S. M. Coxeter, professor of mathematics at the University of Toronto, once called my attention to a geometrical interpretation given to this stanza by the English mathematician John Leech. The stanza tells how to saw and glue together the wooden rods for a model of the skeletal framework of a regular polyhedron. For *locusts* read *locuses* or *loci*; for *tape* read *tape measure*.

The Butcher would gladly have talked till next day,
    But he felt that the Lesson must end,
And he wept with delight in attempting to say
    He considered the Beaver his friend.

While the Beaver confessed, with affectionate looks
    More eloquent even than tears,
It had learned in ten minutes far more than all books
    Would have taught it in seventy years.

They returned hand-in-hand, and the Bellman, unmanned
    (For a moment) with noble emotion,
Said "This amply repays all the wearisome days
    We have spent on the billowy ocean!"

Such friends, as the Beaver and Butcher became,
    Have seldom if ever been known;
In winter or summer, 'twas always the same—
    You could never meet either alone.[56]

And when quarrels arose—as one frequently finds
    Quarrels will, spite of every endeavour—
The song of the Jubjub recurred to their minds,
    And cemented their friendship for ever!

56. I had always assumed that the Butcher and Beaver became a pair of ship buddies until I read Andrew Lang's 1876 review of the *Snark*. "The drawing of the Beaver sitting at her bobbins is very satisfactory," Lang wrote, "the natural shyness of the Beaver in the presence of the Butcher being admirably rendered." The thought that the Beaver might be a "she" is rather startling. Carroll always refers to the Beaver alone with neutral pronouns.

The Beaver's lace making suggests a female, but this is countered by the application of "his" and "he" to the pair, in the fit's third and fourth stanzas. Whichever the case, W. H. Auden, in his book *The Enchafèd Flood* (London: Faber & Faber, 1951), detects an undercurrent of sexual attraction: ". . . the Beaver and the Butcher, romantic explorers though they are, who have chosen to enter a desolate valley, where the Jubjub bird screams in passion overhead, and the creatures from The Temptation of St. Anthony surround them, escape from the destructive power of sex, sublimating it into arithmetical calculations based on the number 3."

Leigh Mercer, the celebrated British palindromist, called my attention in a letter to how the events of this fit contradict the "ever after" in the last stanza of Fit 1.

My statement that Carroll's pronouns do not identify the Beaver's sex was questioned by C. D. Fell in the following poem that appeared in the British journal *Computing*:

I read it through twice, I read it with care,
    I perused it with forks and hope.
I followed its reasons with sympathy rare,
    It charmed me as smiles from a Pope.

Yet with one lone opinion I must disagree
    So I've taken up paper, pen, ink
He says it is plain that the Beaver's a "she";
    Now that is the theory I'll sink.

If you read Fit the Fifth you find him referred
    To not once, not twice, but three times,
By masculine pronouns, so it must be absurd
    To suggest he's a "she" in these rhymes.

In stanza the third of the fit named before
    You'll find the word "his" is applied.
You'll find "he" used twice in verse number
        four.
    If you read it you'll find I've not lied.

You'll find by addition the total is three
    If, you re-read my references through
So the Beaver is male, you must now agree
    For what's said three times is true.

"I must admit to some prejudice in this matter," Fell added. "My father is the Beaver in the Cambridge Snark Club referred to in Martin Gardner's edition of the *Snark*."

I must respectfully disagree with Fell. In all three cases the male pronoun is used not in reference to the Beaver alone, but to both the Beaver and Butcher. It was the custom then to use a male pronoun in such contexts rather than the awkward "his or her" and "he or she."

Fit the Sixth

THE BARRISTER'S DREAM[57]

THEY sought it with thimbles, they sought it with care;
　　They pursued it with forks and hope;
They threatened its life with a railway-share;
　　They charmed it with smiles and soap.

But the Barrister, weary of proving in vain
　　That the Beaver's lace-making was wrong,[58]
Fell asleep, and in dreams saw the creature quite plain
　　That his fancy had dwelt on so long.

57. The farcical side of English law had received its classic expression in 1837 in Dickens's story, in *The Pickwick Papers*, of Mr. Pickwick's trial for breach of promise; a trial that may have influenced Carroll's equally celebrated account of the trial of the Knave of Hearts, perhaps also the Barrister's Dream.

Another possible influence on the dream was the trial of the Tichborne claimant. Sir Roger Charles Tichborne, a wealthy young Englishman, was lost at sea in 1854 when the ship on which he sailed went down with all hands. His eccentric dowager mother, Lady Tichborne, refused to believe that her son had drowned. She foolishly advertised for news of Sir Roger and, sure enough, in 1865 an illiterate butcher in Wagga Wagga, New South Wales, responded. Sir Roger

had been a slim man with straight black hair. The butcher was extremely fat, with wavy light brown hair. Nevertheless, there was a big emotional recognition scene when mother and claimant finally met in Paris. The trustees of Sir Roger's estate were unconvinced. They brought suit against the claimant in 1871, and the trial turned into one of the longest and funniest of all English court cases. More than a hundred persons swore that the claimant was indeed Sir Roger. Lewis Carroll followed the trial with interest, recording in his Diary on 28 February 1874 the final verdict of guilty and the claimant's sentence of fourteen years for perjury.

It is possible that Carroll intended the Barrister's Dream to be a satire on some of the episodes in the Tichborne case, and there is a plausible

He dreamed that he stood in a shadowy Court,
 Where the Snark, with a glass in its eye,
Dressed in gown, bands, and wig,[59] was defending a pig
 On the charge of deserting its sty.

The Witnesses proved, without error or flaw,
 That the sty was deserted when found:
And the Judge kept explaining the state of the law
 In a soft under-current of sound.

The indictment had never been clearly expressed,
 And it seemed that the Snark had begun,
And had spoken three hours, before any one guessed
 What the pig was supposed to have done.

The Jury had each formed a different view
 (Long before the indictment was read),
And they all spoke at once, so that none of them knew
 One word that the others had said.

conjecture that Holiday's Barrister is a caricature of Edward Vaughan Kenealy, counsel for the claimant (see the cartoon of Kenealy in *Punch*, vol. 68, 1875, p. 91). A book on the Tichborne case was in Carroll's library, and he once anagrammed Kenealy's full name as "Ah! We dread an ugly knave."

All this, together with the presence of a Butcher in Carroll's crew, gave rise to a popular interpretation of the poem: that it was throughout intended as a satire on the Tichborne case. (See *The Tichborne Claimant* by Douglas Woodruff, New York: Farrar, Straus and Cudahy, 1957.)

58. See Fit 4, stanza 12.

59. Note the contrast between the appearance of the Snark in "The Barrister's Dream"—thin, with pointed head, ridged back, three fingers, and thumb—and the actual Snark in Holiday's "suppressed" picture (p. 71). Of course the Barrister is only dreaming; also, we must remember that there are several species of Snark.

Bands refers to the traditional pair of projecting cloth strips which you see attached to the Snark's gown below his wig.

John Spencer wrote to me from London: "One small point caught my eye in footnote 51 [of the 1967 Penguin edition]. . . . The 'bands' are described as being attached to the Snark's gown. Barrister's bands which are still worn to this day (such is the readiness of the Bar to move with the times), are separate from the gown and are tied round the neck under a wing collar, taking the place of a conventional necktie. In fact if you look closely at the creature's 'neck' in the drawing . . .

The Barrister's Dream.

"You must know—" said the Judge: but the Snark exclaimed "Fudge![60]
    That statute is obsolete quite!
Let me tell you, my friends, the whole question depends
    On an ancient manorial right.

"In the matter of Treason the pig would appear
    To have aided, but scarcely abetted:
While the charge of Insolvency fails, it is clear,
    If you grant the plea 'never indebted.'[61]

"The fact of Desertion I will not dispute:
    But its guilt, as I trust, is removed
(So far as relates to the costs of this suit)
    By the Alibi which has been proved.

you can make out a bow half way between the wig and the top of the gown. This could be the hanging curl of horsehair sometimes attached to the back of a barrister's wig but I suggest it is probably the point at which the bands are tied on.

"I notice, too, that the gown with its square collar is of the type now worn by Queen's Counsel. Junior barristers wear a different sort of gown, without a collar and made of cotton rather than the QCs' silk. You can be certain of one thing—unless he was properly kitted out the Snark wouldn't have got a hearing before any English judge."

60. "Mr. Burchell," wrote Oliver Goldsmith in chapter 11 of *The Vicar of Wakefield* (1766) ". . . sate with his face turned to the fire, and at the conclusion of every sentence would cry out *fudge*, an expression which displeased us all, and in some measure damped the rising spirits of the conversation."

Fudge (meaning "bosh, nonsense") was at one time a common expression of British sailors. According to Isaac Disraeli (in his *Notes on the Navy*): "There was in our time, one Captain Fudge, a commander of a merchant-man; who, upon his return from a voyage, always brought home a good cargo of lies; insomuch that now, aboard ship, the sailors, when they hear a great lie, cry out '*Fudge!*'"

Thomas Bettler informed me that in the Gilbert and Sullivan operetta *Trial by Jury* (another famous spoof on English courts), the Judge sings:

> Though all my law is fudge,
> Yet I'll never, never budge,
> But I'll live and die a judge!

"Again, it may be remarked," wrote Herbert Spencer in his 1852 essay "The Philosophy of Style," "that when oral language is employed, the strongest effects are produced by interjections, which condense entire sentences into syllables. And in other cases, where custom allows us to express thoughts by single words, as in *Beware, Heighho, Fudge,* much force would be lost by expanding them into specific propositions."

61. *Never indebted,* or *nil debet,* is a legal term meaning "he owes nothing." It is the plea of the

"My poor client's fate now depends on your votes."
    Here the speaker sat down in his place,
And directed the Judge to refer to his notes
    And briefly to sum up the case.

But the Judge said he never had summed up before;
    So the Snark undertook it instead,
And summed it so well that it came to far more
    Than the Witnesses ever had said!

When the verdict was called for, the Jury declined,
    As the word was so puzzling to spell;
But they ventured to hope that the Snark wouldn't mind
    Undertaking that duty as well.

So the Snark found the verdict, although, as it owned,
    It was spent with the toils of the day:
When it said the word "GUILTY!" the Jury all groaned,
    And some of them fainted away.

Then the Snark pronounced sentence,[62] the Judge being quite
    Too nervous to utter a word:
When it rose to its feet, there was silence like night,
    And the fall of a pin might be heard.

defendant, in a common-law action of debt, by which he denies completely the allegations of the plaintiff.

The mathematicians R. M. Redheffer and H. P. Young called my attention to the amusing circular reasoning in the next stanza. Strictly speaking, an "alibi" is an assertion of one's absence from the scene of a crime. The Snark argues that his client is not guilty of desertion because it was somewhere else at the time.

62. Cf. the Mouse's tale in chapter 3 of *Alice's Adventures in Wonderland*, in which Fury (a dog) tells a mouse that he will take him to court and serve as both judge and jury.

"Transportation[63] for life" was the sentence it gave,
  "And *then* to be fined forty pound."
The Jury all cheered, though the Judge said he feared
  That the phrase was not legally sound.

But their wild exultation was suddenly checked
  When the jailer informed them, with tears,
Such a sentence would have not the slightest effect,
  As the pig had been dead for some years.

The Judge left the Court, looking deeply disgusted:
  But the Snark, though a little aghast,
As the lawyer to whom the defence was intrusted,
  Went bellowing on to the last.

Thus the Barrister dreamed, while the bellowing seemed
  To grow every moment more clear:
Till he woke to the knell of a furious bell,
  Which the Bellman rang close at his ear.

63. "Transportation" was the deportation of convicts to a British colony where they were herded into penal gangs and exploited for hard labor. Before the United States won its independence, transported convicts from England provided much of the labor (later taken over by Negro slaves) on the large plantations. Protests from the colonies, chiefly Australia, led to the abandonment of the system, and England began a belated building of adequate prisons. By the time the *Snark* was written, transportation had ceased in England, though it was continued by France and other colonial powers.

Fit the Seventh

THE BANKER'S FATE

THEY sought it with thimbles, they sought it with care;
    They pursued it with forks and hope;
They threatened its life with a railway-share;
    They charmed it with smiles and soap.

And the Banker, inspired with a courage so new
    It was matter for general remark,
Rushed madly ahead and was lost to their view
    In his zeal to discover the Snark.

But while he was seeking with thimbles and care,
    A Bandersnatch[64] swiftly drew nigh
And grabbed at the Banker, who shrieked in despair,
    For he knew it was useless to fly.

He offered large discount—he offered a cheque
    (Drawn "to bearer") for seven-pounds-ten:
But the Bandersnatch merely extended its neck
    And grabbed at the Banker again.

64. The second stanza of "Jabberwocky" refers to "the frumious Bandersnatch," and the White King (chapter 7 in *Through the Looking-Glass*) also speaks of the beast. Eric Partridge thinks the word may combine a suggestion of the animal's snatching proclivities with either *bandog* (a ferocious watchdog) or *bandar* (Hindustani for rhesus monkey).

Without rest or pause—while those frumious[65] jaws
　　Went savagely snapping around—
He skipped and he hopped, and he floundered and flopped,
　　Till fainting he fell to the ground.

The Bandersnatch fled as the others appeared
　　Led on by that fear-stricken yell:
And the Bellman remarked "It is just as I feared!"
　　And solemnly tolled on his bell.

He was black in the face, and they scarcely could trace
　　The least likeness to what he had been:
While so great was his fright that his waistcoat turned white—[66]
　　A wonderful thing to be seen!

65. *Frumious*, another "Jabberwocky" word, is fully explained by Carroll in his preface to the *Snark* (p. 9).

66. Elizabeth Sewell, in her book *The Field of Nonsense* (London: Chatto and Windus, 1952), points out the similarity of this line with a line in an earlier limerick by Edward Lear:

> There was an old man of Port Gregor,
> Whose actions were noted for vigour;
> He stood on his head,
> Till his waistcoat turned red,
> That eclectic old man of Port Gregor.

Note that the Banker's black vest turns white, and his white face turns black. As Harold Beaver observes in his essay "Whale or Boojum," we have here a change from reality to a negative image, so familiar to a photography enthusiast like Carroll. The Banker does not entirely vanish; only his mind vanishes. As Beaver notes, the fate of this crew member, whose name differs from the Baker's only by the addition of one letter, prefigures the total disappearance of the Baker in the next fit.

Leigh Mercer suggested in a letter that Carroll missed a Carrollian whimsy by not having the Baker's shadow, instead of his vest, turn white.

To the horror of all who were present that day,
    He uprose in full evening dress,
And with senseless grimaces endeavoured to say
    What his tongue could no longer express.

Down he sank in a chair—ran his hands through his hair—
    And chanted in mimsiest[67] tones
Words whose utter inanity proved his insanity,
    While he rattled a couple of bones.[68]

"Leave him here to his fate—it is getting so late!"
    The Bellman exclaimed in a fright.
"We have lost half the day. Any further delay,
    And we sha'n't catch a Snark before night!"

67. According to Humpty Dumpty, the word *mimsy* (from the first stanza of "Jabberwocky") is a portmanteau word combining *miserable* and *flimsy*.

68. In Holiday's illustration for this scene we see the Banker, black of face and white of waistcoat, rattling a pair of bones in each hand. In Negro minstrels, popular in Victorian England as well as in the United States and on the Continent, bone castanets were traditionally rattled by Mr. Bones (note the *B*), who occupied one of the end chairs. (Mr. Tambo, who played the tambourine, sat in the other end chair.) Alexander L. Taylor, in his study of Carroll (*The White Knight*, 1952), thinks the Banker's fate "may be a weird caricature of extravagant church ritual," but both Carroll and Holiday obviously had in mind nothing more than Mr. Bones.

At the Banker's feet is a piece of sheet music to be played *con imbecillità*. The Butcher is still wearing the ruff and yellow kid gloves that he put on in Fit 4, stanza 15. The scene has the same gibbering nightmarish quality that pervades the final scenes of the two *Alice* books, just before all the dream characters suddenly vanish away.

Note that the Banker has grown an abundance of hair that is missing from Holiday's first and second pictures.

The Banker's chair, with its helical sides and legs, was common in Victorian England. Chairs almost exactly like the Banker's are in many of Carroll's photographs, including his portraits of Tennyson and Alice's mother.

The Banker's Fate.

Fit the Eighth

THE VANISHING

THEY sought it with thimbles, they sought it with care;
    They pursued it with forks and hope;
They threatened its life with a railway-share;
    They charmed it with smiles and soap.

They shuddered to think that the chase might fail,
    And the Beaver, excited at last,
Went bounding along on the tip of its tail,
    For the daylight was nearly past.

"There is Thingumbob shouting!" the Bellman said.
    "He is shouting like mad, only hark!
He is waving his hands, he is wagging his head,
    He has certainly found a Snark!"

They gazed in delight, while the Butcher exclaimed
    "He was always a desperate wag!"[69]
They beheld him—their Baker—their hero unnamed—
    On the top of a neighbouring crag,

69. The Butcher was thought to be a dunce (Fit 5, stanza 8), but recalling how quickly he recognized the voice of the Jubjub, and how he taught the Beaver more in ten minutes than it could have learned from books in seventy years, it is not surprising to find him making a clever pun. (The Baker's habit of wagging his head when confronted by wild animals has already been men-

The Vanishing.

> Erect and sublime, for one moment of time.
>   In the next, that wild figure they saw
> (As if stung by a spasm) plunge into a chasm,
>   While they waited and listened in awe.[70]
>
> "It's a Snark!" was the sound that first came to their ears,
>   And seemed almost too good to be true.
> Then followed a torrent of laughter and cheers:
>   Then the ominous words "It's a Boo—"[71]

tioned in Fit 1, stanza 12.) The pun reveals great presence of mind on the Butcher's part. The Boojum was undoubtedly so distressed at being unable to see the point of the joke that it was too embarrassed to confront any of the other crew members before they were all saved by the coming of night.

70. "Many children have some fabled ogre," writes Phyllis Greenacre (*Swift and Carroll*, p. 240), "often in animal form, or some 'secret,' with which they scare each other and themselves. This is the antithesis of the imaginary companion whose presence is comforting, strengthening or relieving. Psychoanalysis reveals that it is generally some representation of the primal scene, in which the sexual images of the parents are fused into a frightening or awe-inspiring single figure. This is probably [that word again!] the significance of the *Snark*, in which the last 'fit' is an acting out of the primal scene with the Baker first standing 'erect and sublime' and then plunging into the chasm between the crags."

71. Larry Shaw, in a funny article titled "The Baker Murder Case" (*Inside and Science Fiction Advertiser*, a fan magazine, September 1956, pp. 4–12), argued that the *Snark* is a cleverly disguised tale of the murder of the Baker. On the basis of numerous obscure clues, Shaw proves that the Boots is the Snark, and that the Baker tries to reveal this fact by crying "It's a Boots!" just before the Boots kills him.

Then, silence.[72] Some fancied they heard in the air
    A weary and wandering sigh
That sounded like "—jum!" but the others declare
    It was only a breeze that went by.

They hunted till darkness came on, but they found
    Not a button, or feather, or mark,
By which they could tell that they stood on the ground
    Where the Baker had met with the Snark.

In the midst of the word he was trying to say,
    In the midst of his laughter and glee,
He had softly and suddenly vanished away—
    For the Snark *was* a Boojum, you see.

72. Holiday's illustration for this scene, showing the Bellman ringing a knell for the passing of the Baker, is a remarkable puzzle picture. Thousands of readers must have glanced at this drawing without noticing (though they may have shivered with subliminal perception) the huge, almost transparent head of the Baker, abject terror on his features, as a gigantic beak (or is it a claw?) seizes his wrist and drags him into the ultimate darkness.

The rocks in the foreground, which resemble the back of a prostrate nude figure, add another eerie touch to the scene. Is it my imagination, or do I see a huge face on the largest boulder when it is viewed on a steep slant, with one eye, from a spot below the picture and to the left? Note also the startling resemblance of this picture to Correggio's *Jupiter and Io*, a painting that depicts the naked Io embraced by the green paw of a cloudy Jupiter as he copulates with her.

The "suppressed" Boojum. This Holiday drawing was first published
in 1932 (the centennial of Carroll's birth) in the *Listener* (29 June,
p. 922), and in the *Illustrated London News* (9 July, p. 48).

See the Baker disappear! From a stationery store you can obtain a sheet of red cellophane used for wrapping paper. Place it over the picture. You'll see the Baker vanish before your very eyes! From *The Snark Puzzle Book* by Martin Gardner (Buffalo, N.Y.: Prometheus Books, 1990).

AN EASTER GREETING

WHEN *The Hunting of the Snark* was published close to Easter in 1876, Carroll inserted in each book a three-page tract titled on the first page: "AN EASTER GREETING to EVERY CHILD WHO LOVES 'ALICE.'" The next two pages are reproduced here.

I think we can understand why Carroll did this. He must have been keenly aware that in spite of his constant denials that the *Snark* was anything but nonsense, it was an allegory about the inevitability of death. Now Carroll, a devout Anglican, firmly believed in an afterlife. But there is nary a hint of this hope in the dark stanzas of his ballad. I am convinced that Carroll realized that his poem, though intended to be funny, ended on a note of bleak despair. Because the book appeared near Easter, he saw this as an opportunity to counter the despair with Christian faith; to let his child readers know that when we vanish from the earth we do not vanish from the grace of God.

Carroll inserted his *Easter Greeting* in several of his later books. For a listing of textual variations see Selwyn Goodacre's article "A New Look at Carroll's *Easter Greeting*" in *Jabberwocky*, Summer 1985.

Reactions to the *Greeting*, then and now, couldn't be more at odds. Philosopher Peter Heath called it "Carroll at his sentimental worst." Contrariwise, Goodacre writes: "I find it charming. It moved me when I read it as a child, and it moves me to this day." He cites an often-quoted opinion expressed by Cardinal Newman when he was seventy-five:

The *Easter Greeting* is likely to touch the hearts of old men more than of those for whom it is intended. I recollect well my own thoughts and feelings, such as the author describes, as I lay in my crib in the early spring, with outdoor scents, sounds and sights waking me up, and especially the cheerful ring of the mower's scythe on the lawn . . ."

DEAR CHILD,

Please to fancy, if you can, that you are reading a real letter, from a real friend whom you have seen, and whose voice you can seem to yourself to hear wishing you, as I do now with all my heart, a happy Easter.

Do you know that delicious dreamy feeling when one first wakes on a summer morning, with the twitter of birds in the air; and the fresh breeze coming in at the open window—when, lying lazily with eyes half shut, one sees as in a dream green boughs waving, or waters rippling in a golden light? It is a pleasure very near to sadness, bringing tears to one's eyes like a beautiful picture or poem. And is not that a Mother's gentle hand that undraws your curtains, and a Mother's sweet voice that summons you to rise? To rise and forget, in the bright sunlight, the ugly dreams that frightened you so when all was dark—to rise and enjoy another happy day, first kneeling to thank that unseen Friend, who sends you the beautiful sun?

Are these strange words from a writer of such tales as "Alice"? And is this a strange letter to find in a book of nonsense? It may be so. Some perhaps may blame me for thus mixing together things grave and gay; others may smile and think it odd that any one should speak of solemn things at all, except in church and on a Sunday: but I think—nay, I am sure—that some children will read this gently and lovingly, and in the spirit in which I have written it.

For I do not believe God means us thus to divide life into two halves—to wear a grave face on Sunday, and to think it out-of-place to even so much as mention Him on a week-day. Do you think He cares to see only kneeling figures, and to hear only tones of prayer—and that He does

not also love to see the lambs leaping in the sunlight, and to hear the merry voices of the children, as they roll among the hay? Surely their innocent laughter is as sweet in His ears as the grandest anthem that ever rolled up from the "dim religious light" of some solemn cathedral?

And if I have written anything to add to those stores of innocent and healthy amusement that are laid up in books for the children I love so well, it is surely something I may hope to look back upon without shame and sorrow (as how much of life must then be recalled!) when my turn comes to walk through the valley of shadows.

This Easter sun will rise on you, dear child, "feeling your life in every limb," and eager to rush out into the fresh morning air—and many an Easter-day will come and go, before it finds you feeble and gray-headed, creeping wearily out to bask once more in the sunlight—but it is good, even now, to think sometimes of that great morning when the "Sun of Righteousness shall arise with healing in his wings."

Surely your gladness need not be the less for the thought that you will one day see a brighter dawn than this— when lovelier sights will meet your eyes than any waving trees or rippling waters—when angel-hands shall undraw your curtains, and sweeter tones than ever loving Mother breathed shall wake you to a new and glorious day—and when all the sadness, and the sin, that darkened life on this little earth, shall be forgotten like the dreams of a night that is past!

Your affectionate Friend,
LEWIS CARROLL.

EASTER, 1876.

An Easter Greeting.

PETER NEWELL'S
SNARK ILLUSTRATIONS

P ETER Sheaf Hersey Newell (1862–1924) is now almost forgotten, but in his day he was one of our nation's most popular and prolific illustrator's of books for children. His cartoonish pictures for Carroll's two *Alice* books are reproduced in my *More Annotated Alice* (New York: Random House, 1990), where you will also find a marvelous essay on Newell by Michael Patrick Hearn, best known for his *Annotated Wizard of Oz* (W. W. Norton, 2000) and annotated editions of other classic novels. On the following pages you'll find the three comic pictures Newell drew for *The Hunting of the Snark and Other Poems and Verses* by Lewis Carroll, published in 1903 by Harper and Brothers.

"So they drank to his health, and they gave him three cheers,
While he served out additional rations."

"He would joke with hyænas, returning their stare
With an impudent wag of the head."

"So engrossed was the Butcher, he heeded them not,

As he wrote with a pen in each hand."

A COMMENTARY
BY SNARKOPHILUS SNOBBS

[F. C. S. SCHILLER]

THE following commentary, by the pragmatist philosopher F. C. S. Schiller, originally appeared in *Mind!*, a parody issue of *Mind*, a British philosophical journal. The parody was published in 1901 as a special Christmas number and is believed to have been written almost entirely by Schiller. The year 1901 was a time when the great bugaboo of pragmatism was the Hegelian concept of the Absolute, a concept no longer fashionable in philosophic circles, though it continues to be smuggled into Protestant theology by German theologians with Hegelian pasts.

The frontispiece of *Mind!* is a "Portrait of Its Immanence the Absolute," printed on pink paper, to symbolize the pink of perfection, and protected by a tipped-in sheet of transparent tissue. The editors note the portrait's striking resemblance to the Bellman's map in *The Hunting of the Snark*. Beneath the absolutely blank pink portrait are instructions for use: "Turn the eye of faith, fondly but firmly, on the centre of the page, wink the other, and gaze fixedly until you see It."

It was this comic issue of *Mind* that provided Bertrand Russell with what he once insisted was the only instance he had ever encountered in which someone actually thought in a formal syllogism. A German philosopher had been much puzzled by the magazine's burlesque advertisements. Finally he reasoned: Everything in this magazine is a joke, the advertisements are in this magazine, therefore the advertisements must be jokes. Footnotes to the commentary are Schiller's except for those that I have added and initialed.—M. G.

A Commentary on the *Snark*

by Snarkophilus Snobbs

[F. C. S. Schiller]

It is a recognized maxim of literary ethics that none but the dead can deserve a commentary, seeing that they can no longer either explain themselves or perturb the explanations of those who devote themselves to the congenial, and frequently not unprofitable, task of making plain what was previously obscure, and profound what was previously plain. Hence it is easily understood that the demise of the late lamented Lewis Carroll has opened a superb field to the labors of the critical commentator, and that the classical beauties of the two *Alices* are not likely long to remain unprovided with those aids to comprehension which the cultivated reader so greatly needs.

The purpose of the present article, however, is a more ambitious one. Most of Lewis Carroll's non-mathematical writings are such that even the dullest of grown-ups can detect, more or less vaguely, their import; but *The Hunting of the Snark* may be said to have hitherto baffled the adult understanding. It is to lovers of Lewis Carroll what *Sordello* is to lovers of Robert Browning, or *The Shaving of Shagpat* to Meredithians. In other words, it has frequently been considered magnificent but not sense. The author himself anticipated the possibility of such criticism and defends himself against it in his preface, by appealing to the "strong moral purpose" of his poem, to the arithmetical principles it inculcates, to "its noble teachings in Natural History." But prefatory explanations are rightly disregarded by the public, and it must be admitted that in Lewis Carroll's case they do but little to elucidate the *Mystery of the Snark*, which, it has been calculated,[1] has been responsible for 49½ per cent of the cases of insanity and nervous breakdown which have occurred during the last ten years.

It is clear then that a commentary on *The Hunting of the Snark* is the great-

1. See the Colney Hatch[2] *Contributions to Sociology* for 1899, p. 983.

2. The Colney Hatch Pauper Lunatic Asylum, in Middlesex, was the largest of the mental institutions then serving the London area.—M.G.

est desideratum of English literature at present; and this the author of the pres-
ent essay flatters himself that he has provided. Not that he would wish the
commentary itself to be regarded as exhaustive or as anything more than a *vin-
demiatio prima* of so fruitful a subject: but he would distinctly advance the
claim to have discovered the key to the real meaning and philosophical signif-
icance of this most remarkable product of human imagination.

What then is the meaning of the *Snark?* Or that we may not appear to beg
the question let us first ask—how do we know that the *Snark* has a meaning?
The answer is simple; Lewis Carroll assures us that it not only has a meaning but
even a moral purpose. Hence we may proceed with his assurance and our own.

I will not weary you with an autobiographical narrative of the way in
which I discovered the solution of the Snark's mystery; suffice it to say that
insight came to me suddenly, as unto Buddha under the Bô-tree, as I was sit-
ting under an Arrowroot in a western prairie. The theory of the Snark which I
then excogitated has stood the test of time, and of a voyage across the Atlantic,
in the course of which I was more than tempted to throw overboard all my
most cherished convictions, and I have little doubt that when you have heard
my evidence you will share my belief.

I shall begin by stating the general argument of the Snark and proceed to
support it by detailed comment. In the briefest possible manner, then, I assert
that the Snark is the Absolute, dear to pholisophers,[3] and that the hunting of
the Snark is the pursuit of the Absolute. Even as thus barely stated the theory
all but carries instantaneous conviction; it is infinitely more probable than that
the Snark should be an electioneering device or a treatise on "society" or a poet-
ical narrative of the discovery of America, to instance a few of the fatuous sug-
gestions with which I have been deluged since I began to inquire into the
subject. But further considerations will easily raise the antecedent probability
that the Snark is the Absolute to certainty. The Absolute, as I venture to
remark for the benefit of any unpholisophical enough still to enjoy that igno-
rance thereof which is bliss, is a fiction which is supposed to do for pholiso-
phers everything they can't do for themselves. It performs the same functions

3. A term for Hegelian philosophers, used throughout the comic issue of *Mind.*—M.G.

in philosophy as infinity in mathematics; when in doubt you send for the Absolute; if something is impossible for us, it is *therefore* possible for the Absolute; what is nonsense to us is *therefore* sense to the Absolute and *vice versa*; what we do not know, the Absolute knows; in short it is the apotheosis of topsy-turvydom. Now, Lewis Carroll as a man of sense did not believe in the Absolute, but he recognized that it could best be dealt with in parables.

The Hunting of the Snark, therefore, is intended to describe Humanity in search of the Absolute, and to exhibit the vanity of the pursuit. For no one attains to the Absolute but the Baker, the miserable madman who has left his intelligence behind before embarking. And when he does find the Snark, it turns out to be a Boojum, and he "softly and silently vanished away." That is, the Absolute can be attained only by the loss of personality, which is merged in the Boojum. The Boojum is the Absolute, as the One which absorbs the Many, and danger of this is the "moral purpose" whereof Lewis Carroll speaks so solemnly in his preface. Evidently we are expected to learn the lesson that the Snark will *always* turn out a Boojum, and the dramatic variety of the incidents only serves to lead up to this most thrilling and irreparable catastrophe.

But I proceed to establish this interpretation in detail. (1) We note that the poem has 8 fits. These clearly represent the Time-process in which the Absolute is supposed to be revealed, and at the same time hint that Life as a whole is a *Survival of the Fit.* But why 8 and not 7 or 9? Evidently because by revolving 8 through an angle of 90° it becomes the symbol for Infinity, which is often regarded as an equivalent of the Absolute. (2) The vessel clearly is Humanity and in the crew are represented various human activities by which it is supposed we may aspire to the Absolute. We may dwell a little on the significance of the various members of the crew. They are *ten* in number and severally described as a Bellman, a Butcher, a Banker, a Beaver, a Broker, a Barrister, a Bonnet-maker, a Billiard-marker, a Boots and a Baker. It is obvious that all these names begin with a *B*, and somewhat remarkable that even the Snark turns out a Boojum. This surely indicates that we are here dealing with the most ultimate of all questions, *viz.,* "to be or not to be," and that it is answered in the universal affirmative—*B* at any cost!

Next let us inquire what these personages represent. In the leading figure, that of the *Bellman* we easily recognize *Christianity,* the bell being the characteristically Christian implement, and the hegemony of humanity being equally obvious. Emboldened by this success, it is easy to make out that the *Butcher* is *Mohammedanism,* and the *Banker Judaism,* while the *Beaver* represents the aspirations of the animals towards το Θεῖον.[4] The anonymous *Baker* is, of course, the hero of the story, and the "forty-two boxes all carefully packed with his name painted clearly on each" which he "left behind on the beach" typify the contents of his mind, which he lost before starting on his quest.

The *Barrister* is clearly the type of the *logician* and brought "to arrange their disputes." He too has dreams about the Absolute and wearies himself by proving in vain that the "Beaver's lacemaking was wrong"; as anyone who has studied modern logic can testify, it does dream about the Absolute and is always "proving in vain."

The *Broker* brought "to value their goods" (ἀγαθὰ) is evidently *moral philosophy.* The "*Billiard-marker* whose skill was immense" is certainly *Art,* which would grow too engrossing (= "might perhaps have won more than his share") but for the pecuniary considerations represented by the Banker (Judaism) who "had the whole of their cash in his care."

In the *Boots* we can hardly hesitate to recognize *Literature,* which serves to put literary polish upon the outer integuments of the other intellectual pursuits.

The *Bonnet-maker* finally is manifestly the *Fashion,* without which it would have been madness to embark upon so vast an undertaking.

Having thus satisfactorily accounted for the *dramatis personae* I proceed to comment on the action.

F. 1, st. 1.

> "Just the place for a Snark!" the Bellman cried,
> As he landed his crew with care;
> Supporting each man on the top of the tide
> By a finger entwined in his hair.

---

4. Cp. Aristotle, *Eth. Nich.*, vii, 13, 6.

The meaning evidently is that Christianity "touches the highest part of man and supports us from above."

F. 1, st. 12.

> He would joke with hyænas

It is well known that few animals have a keener sense of humor than hyenas and that no animal can raise a heartier laugh than the right sort of hyena.

> And he once went a walk, paw-in-paw with a bear

The learned Prof. Grubwitz has discovered a characteristically Teutonic difficulty here. In his monumental commentary on the *Shaving of Shagpat*, he points out that *as human* the Baker had no paws and could not possibly therefore have offered a paw to a bear. Hence he infers that the text is corrupt. The "w" of the second "paw" is evidently, he thinks, due to the dittograph initial letter of the succeeding "with." The original "papa" having thus been corrupted into a "papaw" (a tropical tree not addicted to locomotion), an ingenious scribe inserted "w-in" giving a specious but mistaken meaning. The original reading was "papa with a bear," and indicates that a forebear or ancestor was intended. So far Grubwitz, who if he had been more familiar with English slang would doubtless have dealt with the text in a more forbearing and less overbearing manner. Anyhow the difficulty is gratuitous, for it must be admitted that the whole stanza is calculated to give anyone paws.

> "Just to keep up its spirits," he said.

It was probably depressed because it could only make a bare living.

In the second Fit the first point of importance would seem to be the Bellman's map. This is manifestly intended for a description of the *Summum Bonum* or Absolute Good, which represents one of the favorite methods of attaining the Absolute. Moreover, as Aristotle shows, a knowledge of the *Summum Bonum* is of great value to humanity in crossing the ocean of life, although its τέλος is οὐ γνῶσις ἀλλά πρᾶξις.

F. 2, st. 3.

> "What's the good of Mercator's North Poles and Equators,
> Tropics, Zones and Meridian Lines?"

These terms evidently ridicule the attempt made in various ways to fill in the conception of the *Summum Bonum*, but I confess I cannot identify the chief philosophic notions in their geographical disguises.

F. 2, st. 6.

> When he cried, "Steer to starboard, but keep her
>   head larboard!"
> What on earth was the helmsman to do?

The question in the first place is quite irrelevant, as the helmsman was not on earth but at sea and likely to remain there. Still, bearing in mind the effect of this remarkable nautical maneuver, we may perhaps make bold to answer: "He should have turned tail!" For the effect upon the ship would be to make it toss and, as the Bellman obviously preferred the head, the helmsman should have cried "Tails!"

F. 2, st. 9.

> Yet at first sight the crew were not pleased with the view,
> Which consisted of chasms and crags.

When Humanity first really catches a glimpse of the local habitation of the Absolute in the writings of the pholisophers, it is disappointed and appalled by its "chasms and crags," *i.e.*, the difficulties and obscurities of these authors' account.

F. 2, st. 10.

> The Bellman perceived that their spirits were low,
> And repeated in musical tone
> Some jokes he had kept for a season of woe—
> But the crew would do nothing but groan.

Tutors have been known to adopt similar methods with a similar effect.

F. 2, st. 15. We now come to what is perhaps the most crucial point in our commentary, namely, "the five unmistakable marks, by which you may know, wheresoever you go, the warranted Genuine Snarks. Let us take them in order. The first is its taste, which is meagre and hollow, but crisp: like a coat that is rather too tight in the waist, with a flavour of Will-o'-the-wisp."

1. The taste of the Snark is the taste for the Absolute, which is not emotionally satisfactory, "meagre and hollow, but crisp" and hence attractive to the Baker, while the elusiveness of the Absolute sufficiently explains the "flavour of Will-o'-the-wisp." Its affinity for "a coat that is rather too tight in the waist" applies only to its "meagre and hollow" character; for unless the coat were hollow you could not get into it, while it would, of course, be meagre or scanty if it were "too tight in the waist."

> 2. "Its habit of getting up late you'll agree
> That it carries too far, when I say
> That it frequently breakfasts at five-o'clock tea
> And dines on the following day."

In this the poet shows, in four lines, what many pholisophers have vainly essayed to prove in as many volumes, namely that the Absolute is not, and cannot be, in Time.

> 3. "The third is its slowness in taking a jest.
> Should you happen to venture on one,

It will sigh like a thing that is deeply distressed:
And it always looks grave at a pun."

This third characteristic of the Absolute is also found in many of its admirers,
I am sorry to say. It is best passed over in silence, as our author says elsewhere,
without "a shriek or a scream, scarcely even a howl or a groan."

4. "The fourth is its fondness for bathing-machines,
Which it constantly carries about,
And believes that they add to the beauty of scenes—
A sentiment open to doubt."

The "philosophic desperado" in pursuit of Nirvana achieves his fell design
by a purificatory plunge into the ocean of Absolute Being. This, however, is
not an aesthetic spectacle which "adds to the beauty of scenes," and hence the
Snark obligingly carries bathing-machines about in order that in Mr. Glad-
stone's phrase "essential decency may be preserved."

5. "The fifth is ambition." The Snark's ambition is to become a Boojum, of
course. It always succeeds with those who are prepared to meet it halfway. You
will doubtless have noticed that the five unmistakable criteria of Snarkhood we
have just considered are all of a spiritual character and throw no light upon its
material appearance. The reason no doubt is that our author was aware of the
protean character of the Absolute's outward appearance, and with true scien-
tific caution did not pretend to give an exhaustive description of the various
species of Snark. What, however, he does know he is not loath to tell, and so
he bids us distinguish "those that have feathers and bite from those that have
whiskers and scratch." In this it is needless to seek for a causal connection
between the possession of feathers and mordant habits. The fact is simply men-
tioned to distinguish these Snarks from birds which have feathers but—since
the extinction of the *Archaeopteryx* and *Hesperornis*—have long ceased to wear
genuine teeth and to bite, and angels which have feathers but don't bite, not
because they are physically, but because they are morally, incapable of so doing.

Similarly it would be fanciful to connect the scratching, which is attributed to the second kind of Snark, with the possession of whiskers even in an inchoate condition. But *vide infra* for the doubt about the reading.

Let us consider therefore first the information about the outward characteristics of these Snarks. Some have feathers, some have whiskers. There is no difficulty about the former. We simply compare the well-known poem of Emerson on Brahma, in which the latter points out to those who object to being parts of the Absolute, that "when me they fly I am the wings." If wings, then probably feathers; for the featherless wings of insects are utterly unworthy of any kind of Snark.

The mention of Snarks with whiskers on the other hand constitutes a difficulty. For we cannot attribute anything so anthropomorphic to the Absolute. There is, however, evidence of a various reading. The Bodleian MS B$\frac{n}{2}$ 48971, which is supposed to be in the author's own handwriting, reads *whiskey* instead of *whiskers*. The change is a slight one, but significant. For we may then compare Spinoza's well-known views about the Absolute, which caused him to be euphemistically described as "a God-intoxicated man." It should also be remembered that various narcotics such as bhang, opium, hashish, arrack, etc., have been used to produce the mystic union of the devotee or debauchee with the Absolute, and many hold that whiskey is as good as any of them.

It remains to account for the habit of the Snark in biting and scratching. The learned Grubwitz, to whom allusion has already been made, thinks that these terms are intended to indicate respectively the male and female forms of the Snark (who, in his opinion, represents the university student who is capable of becoming a Boojum—a professor causing all who meet him "softly and silently to vanish away"). The demonstrable absurdity of his general theory of the Snark encourages me to reject also Grubwitz' interpretation in detail, in spite of my respect for his learning. I should prefer, therefore, to explain the biting and scratching more simply as due to the bad temper naturally engendered in so inordinately hunted an animal.

The Third Fit opens, as the reader will doubtless remember, with the attempts made to restore the fainting Baker.

> They roused him with muffins—they roused him with ice—
> They roused him with mustard and cress—
> They roused him with jam and judicious advice—
> They set him conundrums to guess

Such as, probably, *Riddles of the Sphinx*.[5] The other means seem to have been injudicious.

Skipping, with the Bellman, the Baker's father and mother, we come to his "dear uncle," who, *lying* on his deathbed, was able to give the important information which has proved so epoch-making in the history of Snarkology.

And first let us ask who was the "dear uncle"? In answering this question we not only gratify our scientific curiosity but also discover the name of the Baker, our "hero unnamed," as he is subsequently (F. 8, st. 4) called. Now, it must be admitted that we are not told the uncle's name either, but I think that from the account given there can be little doubt but that it ought to have been Hegel. Now a distinguished Oxford pholisopher has proved that what may be and ought to be, that ∴ [therefore] is; and so the inference is practically certain.

F. 3, st. 7.

> "He remarked to me then," said that mildest of men,
> " 'If you Snark be a Snark, that is right:
> Fetch it home by all means—you may serve it with
>   greens' "—T. H. Green's[6] to wit—
> " 'And it's handy for striking a light.' "

It is well known that Hegel thought that the *wrong* kind of Absolute (that of the other professors) was "like the night in which all cows are black." It follows that the right kind—his own—would conversely serve as an illuminant.

5. The title of F. C. S. Schiller's best-known book.—M.G.
6. Thomas Hill Green was a distinguished Neo-Hegelian philosopher at Balliol College, Oxford.—M.G.

F. 3, st. 8.

> "'You may seek it with thimbles—and seek it with care;
> You may hunt it with forks and hope;
> You may threaten its life with a railway-share;
> You may charm it with smiles and soap—'"

"You may seek it with thimbles"—this passage is repeated in F. 4, st. 8, by the Bellman, whose subsequent remark in st. 10, "To rig yourselves out for the fight," explains its meaning. Evidently Lewis Carroll here meant subtly to suggest that the pursuit of the Absolute was a form of intellectual *thimble-rigging*.

"You may hunt it with forks and hope." Just as only the brave can deserve the fair, so only the *forktunate* can *hope* to attain the Absolute. There is no justification for depicting Care and Hope as allegorical females joining in the hunt, as the illustrator has done. Altogether the serious student cannot be too emphatically warned against this plausible impostor's pictures; they have neither historic authority nor philosophic profundity. He attributes, *e.g.*, a Semitic physiognomy to the Broker instead of to the Banker; he persistently represents the Baker as clean-shaven and bald, in spite of the statement (in F. 4, st. 11) that "The Baker with care combed his whiskers and hair," and his picture of the Snark exhibits neither feathers nor whiskers! "You may threaten its life with a railway-share." This alludes to the deleterious effect of modern enlightenment and modern improvements on the vitality of the Absolute. "You may charm it with smiles and soap." *I.e.*, adulation and ascetic practices, soap being the substance most abhorrent to Fakirs and Indian sages generally, and therefore suggesting the highest degree of asceticism.

But after all, the momentous revelation of the Baker's uncle is neither his account of the methods of hunting the Snark—they are commonplace enough and he evidently did not choose to divulge his own patent of the Dialectical Method—nor yet his account of the use to which the Absolute may be put—it is trivial enough in all conscience—but rather the possibility—nay, as in the light of subsequent events we must call it, the certainty—that the Snark is a Boojum. No wonder that even the dauntless Baker could not endure the thought that if he met with a Boojum he would "softly and suddenly vanish away," and that the Bellman "looked uffish, and wrinkled his brow." He was of course bound to conceal his emotions and to take an uffishial view of the dilemma. So his reproaches are temperate—

> "But surely, my man, when the voyage began,
> You might have suggested it then?"

> "It's excessively awkward to mention it now—"

F. 4, st. 5.

> "I said it in Hebrew—I said it in Dutch—
> I said it in German and Greek:
> But I wholly forgot (and it vexes me much)
> That English is what you speak!"

The accounts of the Absolute in German and Greek are famous, while the Hebrew and Dutch probably both refer to Spinoza, who was a Dutch Jew, though he wrote in bad Latin. The forgetting to speak (and write) English is a common symptom in the pursuit of the Absolute.

F. 4, st. 14.

> While the Billiard-marker with quivering hand
> Was chalking the tip of his nose.

Art, when brought face to face with the imminence of the Absolute, recoils upon itself.

The argument of the Fifth Fit is broadly this, that the Butcher and the Beaver both hit upon the same method of approaching the Absolute, by way of the higher mathematics, and so become reconciled. Into the reason of this coincidence, and the rationality of this method it boots not to inquire, the more so as it proved abortive, and neither of them was destined to discover the Snark. That they were brought together, however, by their common fear of the *Jubjub Bird* is interesting, and could doubtless be explained if we could determine the meaning of that volatile creature.

Let us ask, then, what is the Jubjub? In reply I shall dismiss, with the brevity which is the soul both of wit and contempt, the preposterous suggestion that the Jubjub is the pelican. But I am free to confess that I have spent many a sleepless night over the Jubjub. Philologically, indeed it was not difficult to discover that Jubjub is a "portmanteau bird," compounded of *jabber* and *jujube*, but even this did not seem at first to give much of a clue to the problem. Finally, however, it struck me that the author had, with the true prescience and generosity of genius, himself stated the solution of the riddle in the line immediately preceding his description of the Jubjub. It is—

Would have caused quite a thrill in Society

It flashed across me that the Jubjub was Society itself, and if I may quote the account of the Jubjub's habits it will be seen how perfectly this solution covers the facts.

"As to temper the Jubjub's a desperate bird,
    Since it lives in perpetual passion:"

This describes the desperate struggle and rush which prevails in Society.

"Its taste in costume is entirely absurb—
    It is ages ahead of the fashion:"

How profoundly true this is! To be in Society this is what we must aim at; we can never be in fashion unless we are ahead of the fashion.

"But it knows any friend it has met once before:"

It is most important in Society to remember the people you have met even once, alike whether you intend to recognize them or to cut them; otherwise vexatious mistakes will occur. There is subtle sarcasm also in the use of the term "friend" to describe such chance acquaintances.

"It never will look at a bribe:"

Such is its anxiety to pocket it.

"And in charity-meetings it stands at the door,
And collects—though it does not subscribe."

No one who has ever had anything to do with charity bazaars can fail to recognize this!

"Its flavour when cooked is more exquisite far
Than mutton, or oysters, or eggs:"

The taste for Society is of all the most engrossing.

("Some think it keeps best in an ivory jar,
And some, in mahogany kegs:")

Some think Society appears to best advantage in an ivory jar, *i.e.*, a "crush" of *décolletées* women, others at a dinner party over the mahogany board.

"You boil it in sawdust: you salt it in glue:"

Dust is American slang for money, so *sawdust* is put *metri gratia* for sordid-dust. That is, Society is boiled, *i.e.*, raised to the effervescence of the greatest excitement, by filthy lucre. "You salt it in glue." *Salt* is short for "to captivate by putting salt on its tail," *glue* is put metaphorically for *adhesiveness*, and the whole, therefore, means that Society is captured by pertinacity.

"You condense it with locusts and tape:"

I.e., lest it should become too thin, you thicken it with parasitic "diners out" to amuse it, and officials (addicted to red tape) to lend it solemnity.

> "Still keeping one principal object in view—
> To preserve its symmetrical shape."

The importance of keeping the proper "form" of Society intact is too obvious to need comment. It is hardly necessary to add also that the reluctance of the Mohammedan and the animal to face a society in which the female sex dominates to such an extent fully explains their common fear of the Jubjub. Lastly it is clear that a word compounded of *jabber* and *jujubes*, the latter being used metaphorically for all unwholesome delights, Turkish and otherwise, is a very judicious description of Society.

The Sixth Fit is occupied with the interlude of the Barrister's dream, which seems to have been prophetic in character and throws further light on the Absolute. That Logic should dream of the Absolute will not of course surprise those who have followed the recent aberrations of the subject. Let us consider then this dream of Logic's.

F. 6, st. 3.

> He dreamed that he stood in a shadowy Court,
> Where the Snark, with a glass in its eye,
> Dressed in gown, bands, and wig, was defending, a pig
> On the charge of deserting its sty.

The pig was probably *Epicuri de grege porcus*, and the charge of deserting its sty was a charge of pig-sticking or *suicide*. For, as the divine Plato excellently shows in the *Phaedo* (62 B), to commit suicide is to desert one's post, and so to desert the *four* posts of the pigsty must be still worse.

F. 6, st. 4.

> The Witnesses proved, without error or flaw,
> That the sty was deserted when found:
> And the Judge kept explaining the state of the law
> In a soft under-current of sound.

The Judge is *Conscience*, the exponent of the Moral Law, noted for its still small voice.

F. 6, st. 6.

> The Jury had each formed a different view
> (Long before the indictment was read),
> And they all spoke at once, so that none of them knew
> One word that the others had said.

The Jury is *Public Opinion* which was evidently (as so often) very much perplexed by the pigculiarities of the case.

F. 6, st. 7.

> "You must know—" said the Judge: but the Snark exclaimed
>   "Fudge!
> That statute is obsolete quite!
> Let me tell you, my friends, the whole question depends
> On an ancient manorial right."

The question was whether the pig was free, or *ascriptus harae*, justly "penned in its pen." In other words, does being born involve a moral obligation to remain alive?

F. 6, st. 8.

> "In the matter of Treason the pig would appear
> To have aided, but scarcely abetted:"

For a soldier to desert his post is, or may be, treason; hence the charge of treason against the suicide.

> "While the charge of Insolvency fails, it is clear,
> If you grant the plea 'never indebted.'"

The suicide is accused of insolvency, of failing to meet the obligations which life imposes on him. His reply is "never indebted," he owes life nothing, he received no "stipend" and will not be "sued for a debt he never did contract."

F. 6, st. 9.

> "The fact of Desertion I will not dispute:
> But its guilt, as I trust, is removed
> (So far as relates to the costs of this suit)
> By the *Alibi* which has been proved."

You prove an *alibi* by not being there. The pig's defence was that it was not there or not all there; in other words, not *compos mentis*. That is, the old excuse of temporary insanity!

F. 6, st. 11.

> But the Judge said he never had summed up before;
> So the Snark undertook it instead,

Conscience has to pronounce judgment upon the particular case, but this particular case has never occurred before; hence Conscience finds itself unable to decide and leaves the matter to the Absolute. The attitude of Public Opinion is similar: "when the verdict was called for, the Jury declined," and "ventured to hope that the Snark wouldn't mind undertaking that duty as well."

In the end the Absolute not only has to defend the offender and take his guilt upon Itself, but also, as ἕν καὶ πᾶν, to assume all the other functions as well, to find the verdict and to pronounce the sentence. Its readiness to do this is suspicious, and suggests the idea that it was acting collusively throughout in pretending to defend the pig.

"So the Snark *found* the verdict," *where* we are not told, but *what* we might have anticipated.

> When it said the word "GUILTY!" the Jury all groaned,
> And some of them fainted away.

The verdict involved a shock to enlightened Public Opinion, like that of the Dreyfus case. The sentence after that seemed comparatively light and so was received with approval.

> "Transportation for life" was the sentence it gave,
> "And *then* to be fined forty pound."
> The Jury all cheered, though the Judge said he feared
> That the phrase was not legally sound.

The sentence was of course absurd, for the suicide had already transported himself out of jurisdiction.

F. 6, st. 16.

> But their wild exultation was suddenly checked
> When the jailer informed them, with tears,
> Such a sentence would have not the slightest effect,
> As the pig had been dead for some years.

The jailer, whose duty it is to keep the pigs in their styes, is the *doctor*. After all, you can do nothing with a *successful* suicide.

F. 6, st. 17.

> The Judge left the Court, looking deeply disgusted:
> But the Snark, though a little aghast,
> As the lawyer to whom the defence was intrusted,
> Went bellowing on to the last.

Though such events shock the Conscience, the Absolute is unabashed.

The Seventh Fit is devoted to the Banker's fate and is perhaps the most prophetic of any. For no discerning reader of this commentary can fail to recognize that it forecasts the encounter of Judaism with Anti-Semiticism. Let us follow the description of this disgraceful episode in contemporary history.

F. 7, st. 3.

> A Bandersnatch swiftly drew nigh
> And grabbed at the Banker, who shrieked in despair,
> For he knew it was useless to fly.
>
> He offered large discount—he offered a cheque
> (Drawn to "bearer") for seven-pounds-ten:
> But the Bandersnatch merely extended its neck
> And grabbed at the Banker again.

The Anti-Semitic Bandersnatch shows that it cannot be bribed by insufficient "ransom," and that two can play at a game of grab.

> Without rest or pause—while those frumious jaws
> Went savagely snapping around—
> He skipped and he hopped, and he floundered and flopped,
> Till fainting he fell to the ground.

After the Anti-Semitic rioters had been driven off, it was found that the Banker—

> . . . was black in the face, and they scarcely could trace
> The least likeness to what he had been:
> While so great was his fright that his waistcoat turned white—
> A wonderful thing to be seen!

This alludes to the wonderful affinity Judaism has for clothing, and we may parallel this passage by referring to Shakespeare's (?) *Merchant of Venice*, Act ii, Scene 1. There an insult offered to his "Jewish gaberdine" produces a powerful emotional effect upon Shylock. Here conversely the ill treatment of their wearer calls forth a sympathetic compensatory effect on the part of the clothes.

In the Eighth Fit the tragedy reaches its consummation and comment is almost needless.

It must be *read*, not without tears, and every line in it confirms the view we have taken of the Snark.

F. 8, st. 5.

Erect and sublime, for one moment of time.

I.e., before becoming a moment in the timeless Absolute.

F. 8, st. 9.

> In the midst of the word he was trying to say,
> In the midst of his laughter and glee,
> He had softly and silently vanished away——[7]
> For the Snark *was* a Boojum, you see.

One can't help feeling a little sorry for the Baker personally, but nevertheless the verdict of Philosophy must be: "So perish all who brave the Snark again!"

---

7. This line is persistently misquoted by Snobbs; the word is *suddenly*, not *silently*.—M.G.

THE CLUE

A SEQUEL BY J. A. LINDON

FIT THE SEVEN-AND-A-HALF

JAMES Albert Lindon, a writer of comic verse who lived in Surrey, England, and whose name has been mentioned many times in the notes, is the author of the following fit. "It is rather disappointing," he writes in a letter, "that we hear so little of some of the other members of the crew. Further, one feels that the violence of the Banker's Fate detracts from the drama of the ending, the Vanishing, which follows it. So, just for amusement, I have concocted an extra fit, which we can imagine as coming between these two concluding fits. It is of average length and (as befits interpolation, and especially one at that point) it is not violent or particularly dramatic. Nobody meets a decisive fate, and neither the balance of the tale nor the general status quo is altered."

Mr. Lindon's fit, first published in my 1962 edition of *The Annotated Snark*, fits so neatly into the spirit of Carroll's agony that I think it provides this fitful commentary with a most fitting conclusion. The footnotes are Lindon's.

The Clue
by J. A. Lindon

They sought it with thimbles, they sought it with care;
    They pursued it with forks and hope;
They threatened its life with a railway-share;
    They charmed it with smiles and soap.

But the Billiard-marker, who'd left on the ship
    All the cannons he'd recently made,
Had wandered apart, with the red in his grip,
    To a spot of convenient shade.

Where, baulked of all hope, he was potting the soap
    With the butt of his thimble-tipped cue.
(In the glummering[1] dark, with no sign of a Snark,
    There was not very much he could do.)

But as he bent, aiming to pocket his care,
    There came a sharp sound in the woods;
And out, all dishevelled, a bow in his hair,
    Flew the maker of Bonnets and Hoods.

He was red with exertion, and blue with the cold,
    He was white with some terror he'd seen;
As the low setting sun turned his feathers to gold
    And his ears a bright emerald green.

He struggled to speak, but emitted a squeak
    Like a bone that has come out of joint.
What on earth had occurred? He had seen—he had heard—
    Not a thing could he do but to point.

The Billiard-marker cajoled him with nods,
    He spun him a kiss off the cush;
He played him a thousand up, giving him odds
    Of nine hundred, not barring the "push."

1. *Glummering*—the sort of gloomy glimmering that makes you glum.

But no word could he say, merely gestured away
    With a frantic but eloquent poke;
So, with tables[2] and chalk, they set off at a walk,
    For the thing was too grave for a joke.

The sunlight was gilding the tops of the crags,
    The gulfs were all shadowed in blue,
As they heard from afar, like the tearing of rags,
    A sound that they both of them knew.

" 'Tis a Snark!" cried the Billiard-marker with glee,
    " 'Tis the voice of a Snark!" he exclaimed;
" 'Tis a Snark! Now the times I have told you are three!"
And with "jump" for a hazard he aimed.

The maker of Hoods, quite approving of that,
    Here showed him a print on the ground:
It was long, it was large, it was dim, it was flat,
    It was gray, it was new, it was round.

" 'Tis the trail of a Snark!" cried the man who would mark
    Up the score and put chalk on the cues.
"More than one has been past—when you meet them at last,
    Snarks are often discovered in twos."

With forks at the ready, impaling their soap,
    With threatening shares and a smile,
They followed the tracks with ebullient hope
    Through the fortieth part of a mile.

2. There was really only one table, but it had a second playing surface underneath, in case it rained. The bowsprit generally wobbled on wet days, because the Billiard-marker used all the ship's glue to keep the balls in position.

Then the maker of Bonnets beribboned his heels,
    Explaining by signs how he'd seen
Other marks, which had surely been made by the wheels
    Of a Snarked-about bathing-machine.

They had come to a place among lowering crags,
    And the sound they were seeking was there:
Like a swishing and scraping, or tearing of rags—
    'Twas the noise of the Snark in its lair!

They rounded a rock, full of joy at the catch,
    And there were the creatures quite plain:
One was turning a grindstone, with whirring and scratch,
    And sucking the crook of his cane.

The other had rolled up the sleeves of his shirt
    And with scraper and brush well aloft,
He was slaving away at removing the dirt
    From a shoe that the Broker had doffed.

Like gold in the sun shone the crags every one,
    Dark-shadowed lay boulders and roots;
From afar in a dell came the sound of the bell;
    They had only been following—*Boots*.

NOTE: Lindon later wrote a full-scale parody of the entire *Snark* ballad. See "The Hunting of the Slype: A Travesty in Late Bits" in *The Worm Runner's Digest*, vol. 11, no. 2, December 1969, pp. 84–97. It deserves reprinting as a book.

"THE SNARK'S SIGNIFICANCE"

BY HENRY HOLIDAY

MUCH fruitless speculation has been spent over supposed hidden meanings in Lewis Carroll's *Hunting of the Snark*. The inclination to search for these was strictly natural, though the search was destined to fail.

It is possible that the author was half-consciously laying a trap, so readily did he take to the inventing of puzzles and things enigmatic; but to those who knew the man, or who have divined him correctly through his writings, the explanation is fairly simple.

Mr. Dodgson had a mathematical, a logical, and a philosophical mind; and when these qualities are united to a love of the grotesque, the resultant fancies are sure to have a quite peculiar charm, a charm so much the greater because its source is subtle and eludes all attempts to grasp it. Sometimes he seems to revel in ideas which are not merely illogical but anti-logical, as where the Bellman supplies his crew with charts of the ocean in which the land is omitted for the sake of simplicity, and "north poles and equators, tropics, zones and meridian lines" are rejected because "they are merely conventional signs." Or, as in the Barrister's dream, where the Pig, being charged with deserting his sty, the Snark pleads an *alibi* in mitigation. At other times, when the nonsense seems most exuberant, we find an underlying order, a method in the madness, which makes us feel that even when he gives Fancy the rein the jade knows that the firm hand is there and there is no risk of a spill, such as seems to be the fate of so many nonsense writers, if we may judge by the average burlesques of the day. Take "Jabberwocky," for instance. The very words are unknown to any language, ancient or modern; but they are so valuable that we have adopted them and translated them into languages, ancient and modern. What should we do

Henry Holiday (photograph by
Swain after Mendoza).
From A. L. Baldry, "Henry Holiday,"
Walker's Quarterly, nos. 31–32,
London, 1930.

without "chortle," "uffish," "beamish," "galumphing," and the rest? The page
looks, when we open it, like the wanderings of one insane; but as we read we
find we have a work of creative genius, and that our language is enriched as to
its vocabulary.

Whether the humour consists chiefly in the conscious defiance of logic by
a logical mind, or in the half-unconscious control by that logical mind of its
lively and grotesque fancies, in either case the charm arises from the author's
well-ordered mind; and we need not be surprised if the feeling that this is so
leads many to look for some hidden purpose in his writings.

The real origin of *The Hunting of the Snark* is very singular. Mr. Dodgson
was walking alone one evening, when the words, "For the Snark was a Boojum,
you see," came spontaneously into his head, and the poem was written up to

them. I have heard it said that Wagner began "The Ring of the Nibelungs" by writing Siegfried's "Funeral March," which certainly contains the most important motives in the work, and that the rest of the trilogy, or tetralogy, was developed out of it; but as this great work, though finished after the publication of *The Hunting of the Snark* (1876), was certainly begun before it, it is scarcely open to me to maintain that the great German master of musical drama plagiarised in his methods from our distinguished humorist.

Starring in this way, our author wrote three stanzas of his poem (or "fits" of his "agony," as he called them), and asked if I would design three illustrations to them, explaining that the composition would some day be introduced in a book he was contemplating; but as this latter would certainly not be ready for a considerable time, he thought of printing the poem for private circulation in the first instance. While I was making sketches for these illustrations, he sent me a fourth "fit," asking for another drawing; shortly after came a fifth "fit," with a similar request, and this was followed by a sixth, seventh, and eighth. His mind not being occupied with any other book at the time, this theme seemed continually to be suggesting new developments; and having extended the "agony" thus far beyond his original intentions, Mr. Dodgson decided to publish it at once as an independent work, without waiting for *Sylvie and Bruno*, of which it was to have formed a feature.

I rather regretted the extension, as it seemed to me to involve a disproportion between the scale of the work and its substance; and I doubted if the expansion were not greater than so slight a structure would bear. The "Walrus and Carpenter" appeared to be happier in its proportion, and it mattered little whether or not it could establish a claim to be classified among literary vertebrata. However, on re-reading the *Snark* now I feel it to be unquestionably funny throughout, and I cannot wish any part cut out; so I suppose my fears were unfounded.

I remember a clever undergraduate at Oxford, who knew the *Snark* by heart, telling me that, on all sorts of occasions, in all the daily incidents of life, some line from the poem was sure to occur to him that exactly fitted. Most people will have noticed this peculiarity of Lewis Carroll's writings. In the thick of the great miners' strike of 1893 I sent to the *Westminster Gazette* a quotation from *Alice in Wonderland* about a mine; not a coal-mine, it is true, but a mustard-mine. Alice having hazarded the suggestion that mustard is a mineral, the Duchess tells her that she has a large mustard-mine on her estate, and adds, "The moral of that is—the more there is of mine the less there is of yours": which goes to the root of the whole system of commercial competition, and was marvelously apt when landowners were struggling for their royalties, mine-owners for their profits, railway companies for cheap fuel, and miners for wages; each for *meum* against *tuum*.

In our correspondence about the illustrations, the coherence and consistency of the nonsense on its own nonsensical understanding often became prominent. One of the first three I had to do was the disappearance of the Baker, and I not unnaturally invented a Boojum. Mr. Dodgson wrote that it was a delightful monster, but that it was inadmissible. All his descriptions of the Boojum were quite unimaginable, and he wanted the creature to remain so. I assented, of course, though reluctant to dismiss what I am still confident is an accurate representation. I hope that some future Darwin, in a new *Beagle*, will find the beast, or its remains; if he does, I know he will confirm my drawing.

When I sent Mr. Dodgson the sketch of the hunting, in which I had personified Hope and Care:

"They sought it with thimbles, they sought it with care;
They pursued it with forks and hope"

he wrote that he admired the figures, but that they interfered with the point, which consisted in the mixing up of two meanings of the word "with." I replied, "Precisely, and I intended to add a third—'in company with'—and so develop the point." This view he cordially accepted, and the ladies were admitted.

In the copy bound in vellum which he gave me the dedication runs: "Presented to Henry Holiday, most patient of artists, by Charles L. Dodgson, most exacting but not most ungrateful of authors, March 29, 1876."

The above instance will show that though he justly desired to see his meanings preserved, he was not exacting in any unreasonable spirit. The accompanying letter [not included here], written after the work was complete, will sufficiently show the friendly tone which had characterised our correspondence.

—*Academy*, 29 January 1898

EXCERPTS FROM
HENRY HOLIDAY'S
Reminiscences of My Life

HENRY Holiday notes in his autobiography, *Reminiscences of My Life* (1914), his first meeting with Dodgson in 1869:

It was an agreeable surprise when one morning Lewis Carroll (the Rev. C. L. Dodgson) came to see me and my work, in company with a friend of his and mine. We became friends on the spot and continued so till his death. He was intimate with Dr. Kitchin and his family, and shared my admiration for the beautiful little daughter, of whom he took photographs at frequent intervals from then till she was grown up. He made a highly characteristic conundrum about these portraits. The girl was called Alexandra, after her godmother, Queen Alexandra, but as this name was long she was called in her family X, or rather Xie. She was a perfect sitter, and Dodgson asked me if I knew how to obtain excellence in a photograph. I gave it up. "Take a lens and put Xie before it." I have a collection of these portraits, all good. (p. 165)

Holiday goes on to describe Dodgson's many visits, and the events that led to the commission to illustrate *The Hunting of the Snark*:

We saw a good deal of Mr. Dodgson (Lewis Carroll) at this time. He stayed with us a week or more in 1875 when he spent most of his time photographing. He had been a week with us at Marlborough Road pursuing the same hobby. On that occasion some of the young Cecils came, the children of the Marquis of Salisbury, Lady Gwendolen, and two of the sons, I think the present Marquis and Lord Robert Cecil.

This time at Oak-Tree House, he took many of his friends, and gave me a complete set of prints mounted in a beautifully bound book, with his dedication, "In memory of a pleasant week." Among others he photographed Miss Marion Terry in my chain-mail, and I drew her lying on the lawn in the same.

Shortly after this he wrote to me asking if I would design three illustrations to *The Hunting of the Snark*, in three cantos, of which he sent me the MS. It was a new kind of work and interested me. I began them at once, and sent him the first sketches, but he had in the meantime written another canto, and asked for a drawing for it; I sent this, but meantime he had written a new canto and wanted another illustration; and this went on till he pulled up at the eighth canto, making, with the frontispiece, nine illustrations.

We had much correspondence of a friendly character over the drawings. I remember that Dodgson criticised my introduction of the figures of Hope and Care in the scene of "The Hunting," on the ground that he had intentionally confounded two meanings of the word "with" in the lines:

"They sought it with thimbles, they sought it with care;
They pursued it with forks and hope,"

where "with" is used in the mixed senses of indicating the instrument and the mental attitude, and he thought I had missed this point by personifying Hope and Care. I answered that, on the contrary, I had particularly noted that confusion, and had endeavoured to make confusion worse confounded by laying yet another meaning on the back of poor "with,"—to wit "in company with." Dodgson wrote cordially accepting this view, so the ladies were allowed to join the hunt.

I have often found an unexpected use for a casual sketch taken without special purpose, and the cover of the "Snark" is a case in point. A year or more after my return from India I had to go to Liverpool on business, and, having become enamoured of the sea on that trip, I decided to go by boat instead of by rail, and I invited Almquist to go with me. I do not recommend this as an economical way of reaching Liverpool, as it took us four days and nights, instead of four hours, with travelling and board for two all the time; but it was very interesting. We went down the Thames, round the Forelands, coasted round the Isle of Wight (where I could recognise all my old haunts of 1852 and 1858) into Plymouth Harbour, round Land's End, along the Welsh coast and all round Holyhead and Llandudno to Liverpool.

At the Land's End I made a sketch which included a bell-buoy, picturesque to eye and ear, with the weird irregular tolling of the bell, and when Dodgson wanted a motive for the back-cover, something that would bear the words, "It was a Boojum," I bethought me of my bell-buoy, which exactly met his want.

SELECTED BIBLIOGRAPHY

Since the first publication of my *Annotated Alice* in 1960 (New York: C. N. Potter) and the publication in 1962 of *The Annotated Snark* (New York: Simon & Schuster), books and articles about Lewis Carroll and his writings, along with newly illustrated editions and translations of his fiction and verse, have proliferated so rapidly that it would require a book to do justice to this vast literature. The selected bibliography that follows is limited to books in English.

Translations of the *Snark*

The appeal of the *Snark* has not been confined to readers of Carroll's original text, for it has been translated into a number of languages. A bibliographical description of those editions, together with a complete bibliography of English editions, follows in Selwyn H. Goodacre's "The Listing of the *Snark*." A sampling of some of the foreign texts, however, is included here, listed in order of their appearance.

La Chasse au Snark. Chapelle-Reanville-Eure, 1929. Translated into French by Louis Aragon.

Aragon wrote this pedestrian translation (it has neither rhyme nor meter) when he was a young Bohemian in Paris, associated with the surrealist movement, and shortly before he completed his transition from Snarxism to Marxism to become the leading literary figure of the French Communist Party.

The first manifesto of the French surrealists, written by André Breton in 1924, spoke of Carroll as a surrealist. In 1931 Aragon contributed an essay on Carroll to the French magazine *Le Surréalisme au service de la révolution*, in which he tried to show that Carroll's nonsense writings, disguised as children's books, actually were politically subversive protests against Victorian bourgeois morality and hypocrisy. The essay is remarkable also for its many factual errors (e.g., the statement that Carroll wore a pointed beard), but there is no evidence that Aragon intended it as a joke. In fact, Breton wrote an article in 1939 to refute Aragon's Marxist interpretation of Carrollian nonsense. (See Philip Thody's essay, "Lewis Carroll and the Surrealists," in the *Twentieth Century*, vol. 163, May 1958, pp. 427–34.)

The following sample stanza from Aragon's translation (as well as the stanzas quoted below from other translations) is the "sought it with thimbles" stanza that begins each of the last four fits.

> Ils le traquèrent avec des gobelets ils le
>   traquèrent avec soin
> Ils le poursuivirent avec des fourches et de
>   l'espoir
> Ils menacèrent sa vie avec une action
>   de chemin de fer
> Ils le charmèrent avec des sourires et du
>   savon

The Hunting of the Snark. London, 1934. Translated into Latin by Percival Robert Brinton, Rector of Hambleden, Bucks, England.

"I have . . . found a certain affinity in character as well as in experience [Brinton writes in his introduction] between the hero of the Aeneid and the hero of 'The Snark.' Both the Bellman and the pious Aeneas were leaders of an adventurous expedition by sea and land: both pursued their quest with simplicity and single-mindedness. Each had devoted followers; each found himself thwarted by a hostile and mysterious power; each has survived to interest later generations in his story."

Mr. Brinton's translation is in Virgilian hexameters:

> Spe simul ac furcis, cura et digitalibus usi
> Quaerebant praedam socii: via ferrea monstro
> Letum intentabat: risus sapoque trahebant.

The Hunting of the Snark. Oxford, 1936. Translated into Latin elegiacs by Hubert Digby Watson. Foreword by Gilbert Murray.

The book includes a note by Watson in which he interprets the poem as a search for world peace. "May not 'thimbles' be an allusion to the 'Women's peace crusade' and 'smiles and soap' to the lip-service of those whose practice seldom comes up to their preaching?" He sees the Baker as a "mild-mannered Pacifist who is on very friendly terms with the (Russian) Bear, but suffers a great shock when the Peace which he thinks he has discovered turns out to be an army entitled 'The International Police Force of the New Commonwealth.' "

The Butcher, in Watson's view, is the "truculent warmonger," the Beaver the isolationist who "displays no interest in the concern" but eventually becomes the warmonger's bosom friend. The voice of the Jubjub is the screechings of the yellow press. And so on. He concludes on a hopeful note: the new Bellman of England, Stanley Baldwin, has a name that begins with *B*.

> Cum cura et digiti quaerunt muliebribus
>   armis,
>   Cum furcis etiam spe comitante petunt;
> Instrumenta viae ferratae scripta minantur,
>   Sapone et fabricant risibus illecebras.

La Chasse au Snark. Paris, 1940. A translation into French rhymed verse by Henri Parisot.

This translation, which Parisot continually revised, appeared in several later editions.

The following stanza is from the ballad's inclusion in Parisot's translation of *Through the Looking-Glass*, published in Paris by Flammarion, 1969.

> Ils le traquaient, armés d'espoir, de dés à
>   coudre,
> De fourchettes, de soin; ils tentaient de
>   l'occire
> Avec une action de chemin de fer; ou de
> Le charmer avec du savon et des sourires.

La Caccia allo Snarco. Rome, 1945. Translated into Italian by Cesare Vico Lodovici.

> Lo cercarono con diligenza, lo cercarono con
>   ditali,
> lo inseguirono con speranza e con forchette;
> gli insidiarono la vita con un' Anzione delle
>   "Meridionali":
> lo incantarono con sorrisi e saponette.

Snarkjakten. Helsingfors, 1959. A Swedish translation by Lars Forssell.

> De sökte med fingerborg, listigt fördrev
>   med såpa och smaskratt dess hopp.
> Av aktieposter de bildade drev,
>   med gaffelskaft drev de den opp.

Snarkejagten. Copenhagen, 1963. Translated into Danish by Christopher Maaløe.

> Så søgte de snarken med gaffel og kiv
>   for at slå den med stumhed og stylter
> og true dens liv med et regulativ.
>   De lokked med smil og med sylter.

Die Jagd nach dem Schnark. Frankfurt am Main, 1968. Translated into German by Klaus Reichert.

> Du suchst es mit Sorgfalt—und suchst es
>   mit Salz;
> Du jagst es mit Hoffnung und Gabeln;
> Du bedrohst seinen Kopf mit der Auerhalm-
>   balz;
> Du bestrickst es mit Seife und Fabeln.

NOTE: A German work with the startling title *Die Fahrt der Snark* (Berlin, 1930) turns out to be a translation of Jack London's book *The Cruise of the Snark*, 1908. This is an account of a voyage that London and his wife made around the world in a small boat which London built himself and named the *Snark* "because we could not think of any other name."

De Jacht op de Trek. The Hague, 1977. Translated into Dutch by Erdwin Spits.

> Zij spoorden met vingerhoed, spoorden met
>   gratie;
> Joegen hem voort met vorken en hoop;
> Zij bedreigden hem met een NS-obligatie;
> Bekoorden met glimlach en zeep.

De Jacht op de Strok. Amsterdam, 1977. Translated into Dutch by Evert Geradts.

> Zij zochten 't met zorg en een vingerhoed;
>   Ze jaagden 't met vorken en hoop;
> Ze brachten 't in 't nauw met Onroerend
>   Goed;
>   Een glimlach met zeep deed 'n hoop.

Contemporary Reviews of the *Snark*

Andrew Lang. *Academy*, vol. 9, 8 April 1876, pp. 326–7.

A generally unfavorable review of both text and pictures. After quoting the stanza about the Snark's slowness in taking a jest and its habit of looking grave at puns, Lang adds: "To tell the truth, a painful truth it is, this quality of the snark has communicated itself to the reviewer."

Unsigned. *The Athenaeum*, vol. 67, 8 April 1876, p. 495.

"It may be that the author of *Alice's Adventures in Wonderland* is still suffering from the attack of Claimant on the brain, which some time ago numbed or distracted so many intellects. Or it may be that he has merely been inspired by a wild desire to reduce to idiocy as many readers, and more especially, reviewers as possible. At all events, he has published what we may consider the most bewildering of modern poems. . . ."

The two reviews listed above, and four others from 1876 journals, are reprinted in full in Morton N. Cohen's article "Hark the Snark" in *Lewis Carroll Observed*, ed. Edward Guiliano, New York: C. N. Potter, 1976.

Other reviews of the *Snark*, all in the spring of 1876, were uniformly negative. "There is neither wit nor humour in the little versified whimsicality, its 'nonsensicalities' fail either to surprise or amuse" (*Saturday Review*, 8 April). "Carroll goes from good to bad, and from bad to worse. . . . This book . . . deserves only to be called rubbish" (*Vanity Fair*, 29 April). "An outright 'failure' without humour" (*Spectator*, 22 April).

Holiday's art took a similar drubbing. "The illustrations display that strange want of any sense of fun. . . ." (*Saturday Review*, 15 April). ". . . by the side of *Alice* [the illustrations] . . . look poor and course" (*Courier*, 11 May).

About the *Snark*

"The Hunting of the Snark." By "Frumious." *The Wykehamist*, May 1876, pp. 2–3. An anonymous commentary in rhymed couplets, reprinted by Morton N. Cohen in "Hark the Snark," in *Lewis Carroll Observed*, ed. Edward Guiliano, New York: C. N. Potter, 1976.

"The Snark's Significance." Henry Holiday. *Academy*, 29 January 1898, pp. 128–30. (Included in this book.)

"A Commentary on the *Snark*." Snarkophilus Snobbs [F. C. S. Schiller]. *Mind!* (a parody issue of *Mind*, published by the editors as a special Christmas number, 1901), pp. 87–101. (Included in this book.)

"The Hunting of the Snark." Devereux Court. *Cornhill Magazine*, vol. 30, March 1911, pp. 360–5.

"Finding of the Snark." Arthur Ruhl. *Saturday Review of Literature*, vol. 9, 18 March 1933, pp. 490–1.

"1874–76—The Hunting of the Snark," chapter 10 in *The Diaries of Lewis Carroll*, ed. Roger Lancelyn Green. New York: Oxford University Press, 1954.

"The Baker Murder Case." Larry T. Shaw. *Inside and Science Fiction Advertiser*, September 1956, pp. 4–12.

"The Hunting of the Snark." Richard Howard. Pp. 773–6 in *Master Poems of the English Language*, ed. Oscar Williams. New York: Trident, 1966.

"Ironic Voyages," chapter 4 in *Nil: Episodes in the Literary Conquest of Void during the Nineteenth Century*. Robert Martin Adams. New York: Oxford University Press, 1966.

"Snark Hunting: Lewis Carroll on Collectivism." E. Merrill Root. *American Opinion*, April 1966, pp. 73–82.

"What Is a Boojum? Nonsense and Modernism." Michael Holquist. *Yale French Studies*, vol. 43, 1969, pp. 145–64. Reprinted in *Alice in Wonderland,* ed. Donald J. Gray, New York: W. W. Norton, 1971.

"On the Hunting of the Snark as a Romantic Ballad." J. R. Christopher. *Orcrist, a Journal of Fantasy in the Arts* (Bulletin of the University of Wisconsin J. R. R. Tolkien Society), Summer 1973, pp. 30–2.

"Hark the Snark." Morton N. Cohen. In *Lewis Carroll Observed*, ed. Edward Guiliano, New York: C. N. Potter, 1976.

"Whale or Boojum: An Agony." Harold Beaver. In *Lewis Carroll Observed*, ed. Edward Guiliano. New York: C. N. Potter, 1976.

Jabberwocky, vol. 5, Autumn 1976, an issue devoted to the *Snark*, with articles by Denis Crutch, Selwyn Goodacre, Brian Sibley, and Ellis Hillman, and reviews by Sibley and J. N. S. Davis of newly illustrated editions of the *Snark*.

"The Snark Was a Boojum." Haydée Faimberg. *International Review of Psycho-Analysis*, vol. 4, 1977, pp. 243–9.

The Hunting of the Snark: Second Expedition. Peter Wesley-Smith, illustrated by Paul Stanish. Camperdown, New South Wales, Australia: Cherry Books, 1996.

The Hunting of the Snark Concluded. Cathy Bowern, illustrated by Brian Puttock. Ryde, Isle of Wight: Angerona Press, 1997. The book includes Carroll's poem, followed by Bowern's eight additional fits.

"The Consumption of the Snark." Ferdnando Soto. *The Carrollian*, Autumn 2001, no. 8, pp. 9–50.

"The Capture of the Snark." E. Fuller Torrey and Judy Miller. *Knight Letter*, Spring 2004, no. 73, pp. 21–5.

About Lewis Carroll

The Life and Letters of Lewis Carroll. Stuart Dodgson Collingwood. London: T. F. Unwin, 1898.

The Lewis Carroll Picture Book. Stuart Dodgson Collingwood. London: T. F. Unwin, 1899. Reprint [titled *Diversions and Digressions*], New York: Dover, 1961.

The Story of Lewis Carroll. Isa Bowman. London: J. M. Dent, 1899.

Lewis Carroll in Wonderland and at Home. Belle Moses. New York: D. Appleton & Co., 1910.

Lewis Carroll. Walter de la Mare. London: Faber & Faber, 1932.

The Life of Lewis Carroll. Langford Reed. London: W. & G. Foyle, 1932.

A Selection from the Letters of Lewis Carroll to His Child-friends. Ed. Evelyn M. Hatch. London: Macmillan, 1933.

Carroll's Alice. Harry Morgan Ayres. New York: Columbia University Press, 1936.

Victoria through the Looking-Glass. Florence Becker Lennon. New York: Simon & Schuster, 1945. Reprint, New York: Collier, 1962.

Lewis Carroll: Photographer. Helmut Gernsheim. New York: Chanticleer Press, 1949.

The Story of Lewis Carroll. Roger Lancelyn Green. London: Methuen, 1949.

The White Knight: A Study of C. L. Dodgson. Alexander L. Taylor. Edinburgh: Oliver & Boyd, 1952.

Lewis Carroll. Derek Hudson. London: Constable, 1954.

Swift and Carroll: A Psychoanalytic Study of Two Lives. Phyllis Greenacre. New York: International University Press, 1955.

Lewis Carroll. Derek Hudson. No. 96 in a series of booklets titled *Writers and Their Work.* London: Longmans, Green, 1958.

Lewis Carroll. Roger Lancelyn Green. London: Bodley Head, 1960.

The Snark Was a Boojum: A Life of Lewis Carroll. James Plysted Wood. Illustrated by David Levine. New York: Pantheon, 1966.

Language and Lewis Carroll. Robert D. Sutherland. The Hague: Mouton, 1970.

Lewis Carroll. Jean Gattégno. Paris: Seuil, 1974.

Lewis Carroll and His World. John Pudney. London: Thames and Hudson, 1976.

Lewis Carroll Observed. Ed. Edward Guiliano. New York: C. N. Potter, 1976.

The Raven and the Writing Desk. Francis Huxley. London: Thames and Hudson, 1976.

The Letters of Lewis Carroll. 2 vols. Ed. Morton N. Cohen with the assistance of Roger Lancelyn Green. New York: Oxford University Press, 1979.

Lewis Carroll: A Biography. Anne Clarke. New York: Schocken, 1979.

Lewis Carroll: A Celebration. Ed. Edward Guiliano. New York: C. N. Potter, 1982.

Lewis Carroll and Alice, 1832–1982. Morton Cohen. New York: Pierpont Morgan Library, 1982.

The Selected Letters of Lewis Carroll. Ed. Morton N. Cohen with the assistance of Roger Lancelyn Green. New York: Pantheon, 1982.

Soaring with the Dodo: Essays on Lewis Carroll's Life and Art. Ed. Edward Guiliano and James R. Kincaid. New York: Lewis Carroll Society of North America, 1982.

Lewis Carroll. Graham Ovenden. London: Macdonald, 1984.

Lewis Carroll: Interviews and Recollections. Ed. Morton Cohen. Iowa City: University of Iowa Press, 1989.

Lewis Carroll. Rev. ed. Richard Kelly. Boston: Twayne Publishers, 1990.

Lewis Carroll in Russia: Translation of Alice in Wonderland 1879–1989. Fan Parker. New York: privately printed, 1994.

The Story of Alice and Her Oxford Wonderland. Christina Bjørk and Inga-Karin Erickkson. New York: R & S Books, 1994.

Lewis Carroll: A Biography. Morton N. Cohen. London: Macmillan, 1995.

Lewis Carroll: A Biography. Michael Bakewell. New York: W. W. Norton, 1996.

Lewis Carroll: A Portrait with Background. Donald Thomas. John Murray, 1996.

Lewis Carroll in Wonderland. Stephanie Lovett Stoffel. New York: H. N. Abrams, 1997.

The Alice Companion: A Guide to Lewis Carroll's Alice Books. Jo Elwyn Jones and J. Francis Gladstone. New York: New York University Press, 1998.

Reflections in a Looking Glass. Morton N. Cohen. New York: Aperture, 1998.

In the Shadow of the Dreamchild: A New Understanding of Lewis Carroll. Karoline Leach. London: Peter Owen, 1999.

Lewis Carroll: Photographer. Roger Taylor and Edward Wakeling. Princeton, N.J.: Princeton University Press, 2002.

Alice's Adventures: Lewis Carroll and Alice in Popular Culture. Will Brooker. New York: Continuum, 2004.

Special mention should be made of the unexpurgated edition of *Lewis Carroll's Diaries*, now in nine volumes, edited and with notes by Edward Wakeling and published by England's Lewis Carroll Society, 1993–1999. The earlier two-volume edition of the diaries, edited by Roger L. Green (London: Cassell, 1953) omitted thousands of entries. Wakeling's newer edition is an indispensible reference for any study of Carroll's life.

About Henry Holiday

"Henry Holiday and His Art." Angus M. MacKay. *Westminster Review*, vol. 158, London, 1902, pp. 391–400.

"The Decorative Work of Mr. Henry Holiday." Unsigned. *International Studio*, vol. 37, New York, 1909, pp. 106–15.

Reminiscences of My Life. Henry Holiday. London: William Heinemann, 1914.

"Henry Holiday." A. L. Baldry. *Walker's Quarterly*, nos. 31–32, London, 1930, pp. 1–80.

Lewis Carroll and His Illustrators. Ed. Morton Cohen and Edward Wakeling. Ithaca, N.Y.: Cornell University Press, 2003.

RECITATIONS AND MUSICAL VERSIONS

Jean Shepherd liked to recite the *Snark* every few years on his New York City radio show. The last time I heard him do this was in 1964. He said his mother used to read the poem to him when he was a child, and that whenever he asked her what a Snark was her reply would be: "It's all in the story." Shep's comment, after he read the final stanza, was: "And that, friends, ain't Uncle Wiggily."

Boris Karloff recorded the *Snark* on a long-playing record released by Caedmon Records in 1959.

On Christmas Eve 1963 the ballad was read by Alec Guinness on the BBC Third Programme, and has since been rebroadcast many times.

The entire ballad, except for the Barrister's Dream, was set to music by Max Saunders and broadcast several times on the BBC Third Programme in the early 1950s. The "sought it with thimbles" stanza was sung as a chorus by a choir of ten men, and the rest of the poem was sung or recited by Michael Flanders to an orchestral accompaniment. Douglas Cleverdon was the producer.

In September 1971 the Whitney Museum, New York City, gave twelve performances of the *Snark*, set to music by Edwin Roberts. The producer was Berta Walker, and the director was Bill Tchakirides. The opera was recorded and broadcast by radio station WBAI on several later occasions.

Laurence Goeghegan's play, based on the *Snark*, was first produced in Bingley, York-shire, in 1949. A musical version, with music by Kenneth Paine, was presented in the Tower Theatre, London, in the winter of 1971–1972, by the Tavistock Repertory Company.

SNARK CLUBS

Snark clubs have flourished at both Oxford and Cambridge, and the Cambridge group still meets in London. The Oxford club, I was told some years ago by Michael H. Harmer, the then Bellman (secretary) of the Cambridge group, was founded in 1879 at New College. Known as The Snarks, it met regularly during the 1880s and 1890s but apparently had its last official meeting in 1914 on the eve of the First World War. In 1952 someone found the club's address book and there was a dinner in London attended by about thirty-five guests, but that was the last gathering of the crew. John Galsworthy and A. P. Herbert were among the distinguished members. The *Observer*, in its color supplement, 8 January 1967, p. 6, printed an 1888 photograph of five members of The Snarks, showing young Galsworthy in the center, sporting a monocle.

The Cambridge group was founded in 1934 by a group of medical students and has been meeting once a year ever since for dinner and a reading of the Agony. It has, at any one time, exactly ten members, each corresponding to a member of Carroll's Snark-hunting crew. William Harmer took over as Bellman after the death of his father (a former member) in 1998. The club's eleven rules are so delightfully Snarkish that, with the Bellman's permission, I reproduce them below:

1. That the Club be called the *Snark Club*.
2. That the object of the Club be the glorification of the Snark and its creator.
3. That an Annual Dinner shall be held.
4. That at each Annual Dinner the *Agony* be read complete.
5. That the fine for nonattendance at the Dinner be a *cheque drawn to bearer for seven pounds ten*, which shall be *crossed*.
6. That any member of the Crew who shall be separated from the scene of the Dinner by not less than *one thousand diminished by eight* nautical miles, be exempt from the fine mentioned in Rule 5.
7. That members be posted in the Agony Column of *The Times* newspaper after nonattendance at the Dinner exceeding two consecutive years.
8.
9. That members be replaced as they *softly and suddenly vanish away*.
10. That the Bellman be responsible for the upkeep of the bell, and that it be his peculiar privilege to tingle same.
11. That *Strange Creepy Creatures* may be admitted as additional members of the Crew from time to time, provided the total number available for Snark service at any one time shall not exceed ten.

In 1972 a club was formed in Newcastle, and continued until members disembarked in 1998. We understand that other clubs may be in existence but prefer to keep their identity confidential.

For a history of Snark clubs, see Selwyn Goodacre's article "On Snark Clubs and Snark Dinners" in *Jabberwocky*, Spring 1994.

THE LISTING OF THE *SNARK*

SELWYN H. GOODACRE *

"... go on with your list ..." (*Through the Looking-Glass*, 1871)

The origin of this section is a booklet I issued on the centenary of the *Snark* inspiration, on 18 July 1974. Subsequently this was developed into the section included in the 1981 centennial edition of *The Hunting of the Snark*, published by William Kaufmann, Inc. I have now updated it to cover the years up to and including 2005.

I am once more indebted to my fellow collectors and enthusiasts who have greatly assisted me in supplying me with details of copies in their possession, and for their further helpful and constructive criticism. In particular I must thank Sandor and Mark Burstein, Joel Birenbaum, August and Clare Imholtz, Charlie Lovett, Yoshiyuka Momma, Mark and Catherine Richards, David Schaefer, Byron Sewell, Alan Tannenbaum, and Edward Wakeling.

The listing is in five sections: English-language editions, translations, anthologies including the entire *Snark*, theatrical and musical adaptations and recordings, and

"candle-ends." The entries are arranged chronologically, but each edition is pursued to its final disappearance, even if the chase extends over forty-two years. Where a description appears meager and hollow, it simply means that darkness came on before a copy was run to earth.

I thank my fellow members of various Snark clubs, in particular the famous Cambridge Snark Club, which finally allowed me to join its illustrious ranks in 1994 as "Boots III," and who annually shudder to think that the chase might fail.

English-Language Editions

1876 Macmillan, London. The first edition, published on 29 March. Dodgson's own copy was dated 30 March 1876, but he inscribed eighty copies for presentation on 29 March. He had earlier thought it would be published on 1 April: "Surely that is the fittest day for it to appear."

* Dr. Goodacre, a British physician who lives in Derbyshire, is a distinguished Carrollian scholar and collector.

The book is fully described in *The Lewis Carroll Handbook* (revised version by Denis Crutch, 1979), but there are two minor errors of description: on the title page, the comma after GLASS should be a period; and the lettering on the spine has periods before THE and after SNARK (as well as between each word).

The basic binding is buff cloth boards (which by now are usually found "weathered" to gray). Dodgson arranged for a number of copies to be bound in special covers: on 21 March 1876 he asked for "100 in red and gold . . . , 20 in dark blue and gold, 20 in dark green and gold, 2 in white vellum and gold." In 1877 he offered a child-friend the choice of light blue or light green.

Edward Wakeling and I have compiled a list of presentation copies and copies in special bindings. At the present count there are fifty-five red cloth copies, of which eighteen have no inscription—which suggests that red cloth copies were offered for sale to the general public as a deluxe alternative to the regular buff cloth.

We have records of sixteen blue cloth copies, and six in green. There is a bit of a problem over the "dark green" and "dark blue" copies as these appear to be very similar—so similar, in fact, that it is nearly impossible to say which is which. Accordingly we have simply identified a further fourteen as being "dark bluish-green." We know of eleven copies in white vellum. In addition we have details of seventeen copies where the binding has not been recorded. It will be appreciated that the numbers we

record bear little relation to the numbers "ordered" by Dodgson on 21 March 1876.

A number of "curiosities" are known—the Harcourt Amory Catalogue (Harvard University) records a copy in "tan cloth, lettered and ornamented in black," and comments that a lavender color is also known. There is known to be a presentation copy in blue and gilt, which has the bell and sail only, on the front cover, with bell buoy on the back.

Four copies are known in dust wrappers. Two of the copies are in red cloth, two in the standard buff. The front cover of the wrapper has a reproduction of the title page; the spine has the title in roman uppercase, lettered upward; the back cover has the Macmillan advertisements for books by Lewis Carroll; and the text on both covers is within a line frame around the border.

The first edition consisted of ten thousand copies, and many are found with *An Easter Greeting* (issued Easter 1876) loosely inserted. It is possible that all copies originally had them. Easter Sunday in 1876 was on 16 April.

Early reprints have the number of "thousand" on the title page. The first reprint was in May 1876. Copies are identical to the first edition, apart from respacing on the title page to accommodate the number of thousand (below HENRY HOLIDAY) in thick black lowercase. Copies have been seen with "Eleventh," "Twelfth," "Thirteenth," "Fourteenth," and "Fifteenth."

The second reprint was in December 1876. Copies now have the number of thousand in uppercase italics, in the same position. The reprint includes the "Sixteenth," "Seventeenth," and "Eighteenth" thousands. During the issue of this reprint, the binding style changed from the buff cloth to a red binding similar to that of the Alice books— cloth boards, with three parallel lines around the border and gilt roundels on the front and back covers, the front with the Bellman and the back with the Beaver, the latter being slightly smaller in size. Copies of the "Seventeenth" thousand are known in both styles. The price rose from 3/6 to 4/6 in 1877, probably coincidental with the change in binding.

Stocks remained available for sale until 1883, when they were withdrawn because of the publication of *Rhyme? And Reason?* (which included the full text and pictures of the *Snark*).

In 1890 the *Snark* was readvertised. Remaining bound copies of the "Eighteenth Thousand" were sold off first. The new issue was bound in red cloth boards, decorated and lettered in gilt in a return to the pictorial design of the first edition. The first issue, styled "Nineteenth Thousand," appeared in July 1890. Thereafter the date of reprint appears on the reverse of the title page—the first in December 1890. Reprints followed in 1891, 1893, 1894, 1895, and 1896. For the first reprint of 1897, the height was increased slightly (from 18.5 to 18.7 cm) to match the similar increase in height of the new editions of the Alice books of 1897.

Reprints followed in 1897, 1898, 1899, 1900, 1903 (when the endpapers changed from black to white), 1906, 1908, and 1910. Advertisements in other Carroll works give varying numbers of thousand for the edition as the years go by, but no great reliance can be placed on these numbers. For example, "20th Thousand" is quoted in 1897 and also in 1908, whereas other 1908 advertisements state "25th Thousand."

The price remained at 4/6 until 1918 when it rose to 6/-. The edition finally went out of print in 1920, just over forty-two years after it was first published.

Many of the reprints will have had dust wrappers, but examples are rare. A 1908 reprint example has been seen: a speckled yellow paper covered with a close design based on the Macmillan motif in orange. The title is in black, with an elaborate Macmillan motif in black in the center; title, etc., on the spine; and the back with the advertisements, flaps blank.

1876 James R. Osgood, Boston. A curious production, presumably pirated, and probably produced by a photographic process from a copy of the English edition, which it mimics closely apart from being very small. Buff paperboards, paler yellow end papers. Pp. xiv, 86. 13.2 × 8.6 cm. Reprinted in 1877.

1890 Macmillan, New York. Possibly timed to coincide with the new reprint in England. The binding is similar to the English edition—red cloth—but the pictures and lettering are in black. Reprinted in 1891.

(1896) A. L. Burt, New York. In copies of *Through the Looking-Glass*, in The Little

Women Series and The Wellesley Series for Girls, the *Snark* appears on pp. 183–226.

1897 Van Vechten & Ellis, Wausau, Wisconsin. A limited edition of ninety-nine numbered copies. Vellum boards, decorated in red and black; dredges uncut. The text is printed in black with wide red decorative borders. William H. Ellis contributes "A Word by Way of Palliation," "Explanatory Diagrams and Picturings by Gardner C. Teall." This fine volume was the second book to be issued by the Philosopher Press, "finished on this ninth day of June" but published in November.

There is a cheaper edition, issued at the same time, limited to 333 numbered copies. Beige paperboards, title, etc., and picture within a frame in dark brown on both covers. The text lacks the wide decorative borders. Pp. 88. 15.6 × 12 cm.

1898 Macmillan, New York. Plain red cloth boards, title in gilt on the spine reading up. The covers have a single line around the border in blind. All edges plain, white endpapers, no advertisements. Printed on one side of the leaf only; 52 leaves. The set-up of type is from *Rhyme? And Reason?* 18.6 × 12.3 cm.

Reprinted in 1899, 1902 (when the title on the spine reads down), 1908, 1914 (the copy examined is in green cloth, with title and design on front in white, a white line round the border, title, etc., on spine in white, back blank; this may be a variant), 1922, 1923, 1927, 1930 (the copy seen has title and author

on front cover in blind), and 1937. Thus, just about forty-two years in print.

1899 A. L. Burt, New York. The *Snark* occupies pp. 1–48 (with the Holiday illustrations), and selections from *Sylvie and Bruno* occupy pp. 49–206. Pp. 206 plus two leaves and advertisements. Possibly reprinted in 1910, but no details available.

1903 Harper and Bros., New York and London. Full title *The Hunting of the Snark & Other Poems and Verses.* Illustrations by Peter Newell in sepia monochrome, frontispiece in color. Cream vellum boards, decorated and lettered in gilt; embossed gilt Bellman on the lower front cover. Top edge gilt, others uncut. The *Snark* is on pp. 5–41, with eight pictures (including the frontispiece). The text pages have a wide decorative border in pale green, by Robert Murray Wright.

Issued in a green dust wrapper, with the same design on the front as the front cover; possibly originally issued in a cloth board slipcase, in quarter vellum with gilt title. The Harcourt Amory Catalogue, apparently describing this edition, suggests that it should be enclosed in an oilpaper wrapper lettered on the spine, with "Price $3.00 net." Pp. xiv, 248. 22 × 14.5 cm.

There are two other issues—in green ribbed cloth boards and in red cloth boards.

It seems likely that there was also an issue to match the Peter Newell Edition of the Alice books—black cloth boards with paste-on color picture and title on the front cover. This could be the 1906 reprint.

Another issue was in the Harper's Young People Series, 1903. Green cloth boards with title and figure in red, within decorated border of characters; text printed without ornamental borders; 17.3 × 12 cm. "There was also an issue in blue cloth boards, lettered in dark blue; 16.8 × 11.8 cm. Another issue is in green boards, but not in the Young People Series.

1906 G. P. Putman & Sons, Knickerbocker Press, New York and London. In the series Ariel Booklets. Limp red leather with title in gilt within an ornamental surround; gilt ornamentation also around the border; back blank, the spine with the title, etc., in gilt. Includes the Holiday illustrations (which are attributed to Swain!); also includes poems from the Alice books (with Tenniel pictures) and from other works. Pp. xi, 124. 13.8 × 9.5 cm.

1909 Altemus, Philadelphia. In the Slip-in-the-Pocket Classics series and listed in the *Publishers' Trade List Annual* for 1909–13, 1916, and 1921, although actual copies simply give the copyright date of 1909. A floral design frames the cover design; the series name is printed on the front cover and spine of the dust wrapper. Bindings vary; one is known with a paste-on picture of a landscape signed "J. C. Claghorn." Another copy has been seen in green cloth boards, title and author on the front cover in gilt in an elaborate floral design, title on the spine in gilt, back blank. Pp. 120 plus three blank leaves at the front and two at the back. 13.1 × 10.2 cm.

Also known in the Langhorne Series—"Velvet Calf, Gilt top, Boxed, 75c."

1910 Macmillan, London. The Miniature Edition, published in October, in the same format as the Miniature Editions of the Alice books (1907 and 1908). Red cloth boards, the front cover with the Bellman roundel in gilt, a little above center; the back cover is blank; the three parallel lines around the boarders are in blind, but in gilt on the spine; title and publisher in gilt on the spine. Issued in a dust wrapper, very similar in design to the examples found on some of the contemporary reprints of the standard edition (see above)—speckled yellow paper covered with a close design in orange based on the Macmillan motif, with lettering in black; the back cover has the advertisements; flaps blank. Pp. xiv, 84, leaf with advertisements. 15.4 × 9.9 cm.

Reprinted in November 1910, 1911, 1913, 1916, 1920, 1924, 1928, 1931, and 1935. The first-edition style of dust wrapper was retained at least until the 1916 reprint. The 1931 reprint dust wrapper is in blue on a white paper; the front cover has the Bellman roundel, the back the advertisements, the flaps blank. The dust wrapper for the 1935 reprint is in red on white; the front cover has the illustration for the Baker's Tale, the back is blank, the front flap has the advertisements, the back flap is blank.

As with the standard edition, no great reliance can be placed on the number of thousand stated in the various advertisements. In November 1910 it reads "10th thousand," 1911 "15th thousand," 1913 "20th thousand"; by 1918 it is consistently "20th thousand," but thereafter the number is no longer stated.

The price of the first edition was 1s. In 1918 it rose to 1/6; in 1921 to 2s; in 1942 to 2/6. It was last advertised in 1948, four years short of forty-two years in print.

The 1928 issue was the first where an alternative binding was offered—écrasé morocco, at 5s. This is in blue morocco with covers blank; title, etc., on the spine in gilt. The 1928 and subsequent issues were also offered in "ledura leather cloth," at 3s (rising to 3/6 in 1942). This is yellow, with the same roundel in gilt with three slightly elaborated yellow bands in blind around. Title, etc., on the spine in gilt, with embossed ship, back blank.

It seems likely that the ledura versions were issued in a glassine "transmatic" dust wrapper; these consist of a transparent plastic jacket with printed paper flaps. It appears to be a Macmillan invention, as examples of the 1928 transmatic jacket have a printed note "patent appl'd for"; later examples have a patent number.

(1927) Kahoe and Spieth, Yellow Springs, Ohio. Unillustrated. Marbled paperboards, with paper label on spine with title in black. Pp. vi, 58 (last three leaves blank). 17.3 × 11 cm.

(1932) Peter Pauper Press, New Rochelle, New York. Illustrated by Edward A. Wilson. Green, beige, and brown decorated paperboards, green cloth spine with title and

motifs in gilt. A limited issue of 275 unnumbered copies, printed at the Walpole Printing Office on a green-tinted paper. A picture begins each fit and has block coloring, the color changing for each fit. Pp. 80. 25.1 × 15.7 cm.

A single-leaf prospectus was issued, printed on the same green paper and carrying one of the pictures. 25.1 × 15.9 cm.

Undated (circa # 1930s?) Haldeman-Julius Company, Girard, Kansas. Number 989 in the series Little Blue Books, edited by E. Haldeman-Julius. Unillustrated. Pale blue paper wrapper, lettered in black, Pp. 32. 12.5 × 8.7 cm.

(1939) Peter Pauper Press, Mount Vernon, New York. Illustrated by Cobbledick. Decorated green paperboards; issued in a slipcase. Pictorial title page in green, sepia, and black. Each page is decorated in green and sepia. Pp. 75. 19.5 × 14.0 cm.

There is another issue, also undated. Limited to 1,450 unnumbered copies. Gray paperboards, with darker gray postage-stamp-size illustrations of the characters. Black on red paper label on the spine with the title. Bottom edges uncut. Pictorial title page in red, gray, and black. Each page decorated, the colors changing in rotation for each fit—gray/red; gray/green; gray/orange; gray/blue. Issued in a red paperboards slipcase. Pp. 78. 20.1 × 13.5 cm.

1939 Oxford University Press, London. Full title *The Hunting of the Snark and Other Verses.* Number 2 in the series Chameleon

Books. Unillustrated, but the black front end-papers carry a picture of seven of the crew in black line on white, colored with brown, and the back endpaper Alice and characters from the Alice books, both by Malcolm Easton. Paperboards decorated with a design of fish in brown and gray; title, etc., in gray on the front cover and spine. Issued in matching dust wrapper; the title here is given as *The Hunting of the Snark & Other Lewis Carroll Verses*. The other verses are from the Alice books and *Sylvie and Bruno*. Pp. 64. 18 × 12.4 cm.

Reprinted in 1946 (where the first edition is said to be 1940) and 1949.

1941 Chatto & Windus, London. Illustrated by Mervyn Peake. Yellow paperboards, the front cover reproducing in black the title and picture from p. 19, the back cover the illustration from p. 26, with title above and refrain verse and publisher below; title on the spine in black. Number 26 in the series Zodiac Books. Published on 20 November 1941, at 1s. pp. 48. 18 × 11.3 cm.

Second impression, 1941. Pink cloth boards, with title on the spine in gilt. Issued in a gray dust wrapper, which repeats on the front the title-page design but without the date; the back has the p. 40 illustration enlarged, with publisher's name. Title, etc., on the spine. 20.8 × 13 cm. The text and pictures are identical to the first edition, except for the title page where both are increased in size. This deluxe issue was published on 16 December 1941, at 5s; 1,400 unnumbered copies were printed.

Third impression, 1942. Styled "Second Impression" (on the title page reverse).

Fourth impression, 1948. Very similar to the first, but no mention of previous issues. Published by Lighthouse Books Ltd. and distributed by Chatto & Windus. On p. [47] the *Snark* is listed as Number 4 in a list of six titles. In the series Zodiac Books. Name of publisher is removed from the back cover; price "2s." added.

Fifth impression, 1953. Styled "Fourth Impression." Blank yellow paperboards simulating cloth, with title and publisher's device on the spine in gilt. Issued in a dust wrapper that copies the binding of the first edition, but with nothing below the refrain on the back. 18.5 × 12.3 cm.

Sixth impression, 1958. Styled "Fifth Impression."

Seventh impression, 1960. A special issue for the Reprint Society Book Club. Slightly smaller than the 1953 and ensuing impressions—18.2 × 12.2 cm. The reverse of the title page has "This edition published by the Reprint Society Ltd. by arrangement with Chatto & Windus Ltd. 1960." Limp beige cloth. Front cover has in black the title, author, illustrator, and part of the p. 45 illustration; back cover has the title, etc., and p. 10 illustration, with note of the Book Society.

Eighth impression, 1964. Styled "Sixth Impression." As the sixth, with price (5s. net) added on the front flap of the dust wrapper.

Ninth impression, 1969. Styled "Fourth Impression," but giving a list of impressions from 1953; standard book number added and also on the front flap with the new price (10/-net 50p).

Tenth impression, 1973. Styled "Fifth Impression," but including a bibliographical listing back to the first edition of 1941. Date deleted from title page.

Eleventh impression, 1975. Styled "Sixth Impression." There is a note at the bottom of the tile page reverse that the illustrations are "c Maeve Peake 1941." The dust wrapper has the title running down the front free edge, with note of illustrator at the bottom left. The front flap has the title and illustrator, picture of the Beaver, and price change to 70p net.

Twelfth impression, 1981. Styled "Seventh Impression." Price change to £1.95 net.

"Eighth," "ninth," "tenth" impressions not seen.

"Eleventh impression," 1988. Blue paperboards in a blue dust wrapper, with new design.

Pocket Library, 1993. Glazed paperboards, yellow cloth spine. 14.4 × 11.6 cm. No price stated.

Reissue 2000, with suite of working drawings. Maroon paperboards, lettered in spine in silver. In dust wrapper. Pp. 70. 19.9 × 12.6 cm. Price £9.99.

(1952) **Peter Pauper Press, and Mayflower Publishing Co., and Vision Press, New York.** The cover title is *The Hunting of the Snark, and Other Nonsense Verse*; the other verses are from the Alice books and *Sylvie and Bruno*. Illustrations by Aldren Watson. There appear to be two issues of this volume. The standard edition has a picture at the head of each fit in green. Bound in yellow paperboards, with a fish design, title on upper half of front cover in yellow oblong in a frame; title on spine in yellow on pink; issued in a blue-green slipcase with yellow label with title, etc., and extra picture in green. Pp. 92, 22.4 × 13.6 cm. Also issued as a Collector's Presentation Edition (not seen).

1962 Simon & Schuster, New York (also issued by Bramhall House). *The Annotated Snark,* introduction and notes by Martin Gardner. Buff half-cloth, dark brown paperboards, with gilt bell on the lower front cover, spine lettered in brown. Cream dust wrapper, with title, etc., in red, black, and brown, all within a frame of the Bellman's map. The back has laudatory extracts from reviews of *The Annotated Alice*. Pp. 112. 25 × 14.8 cm.

This book, which contains the full text, copious annotations, bibliography, Holiday illustrations, and appendixes, has been rightly called the "apotheosis of Snarkolatry." The 1981 Kaufmann edition and the present volume are the revised and augmented developments of this book (for details, see below).

First published in England by Penguin Books Ltd., London, 1967. It contains a new preface by Martin Gardner, the entire book revised, updated, and new material added. Paper wrappers, with a pictorial cover designed by Germano Facetti, using six of the Holiday illustrations. The back cover has a two-verse parody about the book.

Reprinted in 1973, with revisions and extended bibliography. Also new wrappers designed by David Pelham, in pale blue featuring on the front cover in brown the title and the Holiday picture of the Bellman supporting the Banker, the upper half against a turquoise circle; the back cover has the same circle, with parody and text as before. Reprinted in 1975 (where it states that the 1973 reprint was in 1974) and again in 1977, and 1979 with further small corrections. And in 1984 (where the 1974 reprint is said to be 1980), and again in 1987. Reprinted several times with the 1974 date and changes in coding. Reissued in 1995 with a new design as part of Penguin Classics, and subsequent changes in coding.

1966 Pantheon Books, New York. Illustrations by Kelly Oechsli, in line from pen-and-ink drawings, with added color wash. Black half-cloth, buff paperboard; title on the spine in gray. Dust wrapper in white, with an extra picture on the front cover against a blue background of the ship in sail approaching; the back cover has the ship viewed sailing away. Pp. iii, 48. 25.5 × 17.5 cm.

1966 De Roos, Utrecht. Illustrations by Peter Vos. An edition specially prepared for members of De Roos, Utrecht, limited to 175 numbered copies on paper made by Hahnemuhle, bound by Proost and Brandt, n.v. Amsterdam. Paperboards with illustrations in monochrome extending over both covers; title on spine in silver. All edges plain. Pp. 40. 25.3 × 17.2 cm.

1968 Manus Press, Stuttgart. Eleven lithographs in color, seven hors-texte; one in black and ten in negative by Max Ernst. Portfolio, in publisher's slipcase. Limited to thirty-three signed copies with an extra suite of twelve signed and numbered lithographs on Japon, and 130 copies signed and numbered on Papier Arches (no extra suite). Pp. 100. Copies of this astonishing tour de force fetch huge prices on the rare occasions they reach auction.

1960s J. L. Carr, Kettering. Illustrated by J. L. Carr; undated. Pale brown and white covers, text on white paper. There was a later reprint in purple and white card covers, with text on pale blue paper; another in blue and mauve glazed card covers, with text on blue paper. Pp. 16. 12.5 × 92 cm.

1970 Heinemann, London. Illustrated by Helen Oxenbury; in color and monochrome. Pictorial paperboards, in green, lettered in white and turquoise, with the picture from p. 29 in a circle, with added color and background. The back cover has the Jubjub from p. 33, again in full color. Marching dust wrapper; back flap has a photograph of Oxenbury and reviews. Issued at 22s. (£1.10). Pp. 48. 27.8 × 21.3 cm.

Published in the same year in New York by Franklin Watts, in identical format at $4.95.

Reissued in 1983 in laminated pictorial boards as the first-edition cover.

1973 Simon & Schuster, New York. *The Snark Puzzle Book* by Martin Gardner. Yellow cloth boards, with bird (from the back cover of the first edition, but in reverse) in black on the upper front cover; title in black on the spine. Pale green dust wrapper, with title based on the Holiday bell-buoy design, on a turquoise background; title on the spine in brown, green, and black. Includes all the Holiday pictures and seventy-five "Snarkteasers," with answers proved in the appendix. "Jabberwocky" also included with the Tenniel pictures. Pp. 138 (last two leaves blank). 23.6 × 16.7 cm. Price $5.95.

1973 Normal, Illinois. Illustrations by Arlene Bennett. Twenty-six unnumbered pages of hand-lettered text with fourteen pictures ranging from tiny marginalia to half-page illustrations. Limited edition of sixty-five numbered copies, signed by the illustrator; hand bound under the guidance of Oliver Fancher at Illinois State University.

1974 Catalpa Press, London. Illustrations by Byron Sewell, introduction by Martin Gardner. Black cloth boards, with pocket inside back cover enclosing cards with sections of the crew members' faces, so that they can be resorted. A limited issue of 250 numbered copies signed by the illustrator. A highly elaborate version; a section of the sheets is given over to a picture of the vessel and crew in a single concertinaed sheet. There are other special effects, which altogether make a page count misleading, if not impossible. 30.2 × 21 cm. Issued at £25. A single-leaf prospectus was issued; 20.8 × 14.8 cm.

1975 The Whittington Press, Andoversford. Line illustrations by Harold Jones. A limited edition of 750 numbered copies signed by the illustrator, including thirty bound in full leather. Black cloth boards (or leather) with title in gilt on the front cover within an ornamental frame; title, publisher's mascot, and four sets of double lines

in gilt on the spine. Top edge gilt; others uncut, a fine and luxurious production. Pp. 48. 29 × 19 cm. Issued at £15 (£30 for the leather copies).

1975 Michael Dempsey, London. Monochrome illustrations by Ralph Steadman. Plain beige cloth boards; title in black on the spine. Yellow dust wrapper with title in illustrator's script with the picture from p. 37. Pp. 72. 27.9 × 26 cm. Issued at £4.50. One hundred fifty copies included an etching, numbered and signed by the artist.

Six of the pictures were issued, in sixty-five numbered sets, in a portfolio of etchings printed by Cliff White of White Ink Limited, signed and titled by the artist, at £150. The book was published in New York by Clarkson Potter in 1976, in gray paper wrappers; front cover has the picture from p. 37 with title, etc., in black and white; back cover has account of the book, author, and illustrator. 27.5 × 25.7 cm.

1976 John Minnion, London. Line illustrations by John Minnion. Blue paper wrappers. The front cover has, in black, the title and an extra picture, the back cover another extra picture, with short biographical note. Pictures on every page interwoven with text in the illustrator's own script. A personal tour de force. Pp. 39. 29.5 × 21 cm. Issued at £1.50.

1976 Folio Society, London. Illustrations by Quentin Blake. Cloth boards, with an extra color picture of the chase extending over both covers. Title in gilt on the spine.

Text set in Bell type, appropriately. Issued in a pale blue paperboards slipcase. Available to members of the society at £3.95. Pp. 52. 22.1 × 15.5 cm.

1980 Windward (W. H. Smith), Leicester. A facsimile of the 1876 first edition. Cream paperboards, with first-edition cover designs in black; the spine has the publisher and title in roman uppercase reading upward, black endpapers. Pale brown dust wrapper with matching designs in dark brown. The spine has the title reading downward; the front flap has text about the volume, the back flap a brief Carroll biography. Issued at £2.95. Pp. xiv, 83. 18.6 × 12.3 cm.

American issue published by Mayflower Books, New York, identical to the above, apart from the publisher on the title page and wording on the title page reverse, and change of publisher on the dust wrapper and spine. Issued at $7.95.

1981 Barbara J. Raheb, Tarzana, California. One unsigned illustration. Edition limited to three hundred copies, signed by the publisher. Blue paperboards lettered and decorated in gilt. Miniature edition. 2.2 × 1.5 cm.

1981 William Kaufmann, Inc., in cooperation with Bryn Mawr College Library, Los Altos, California. Lewis Carroll's "The Hunting of the Snark," illustrated by Henry Holiday. Centennial edition, edited by James Tanis and John Dooley. This fine volume, printed by the Stinehour Press, includes a complete facsimile of the first edition, followed by the full

text again—with annotations by Martin Gardner, an essay "The Designs for the Snark" by Charles Mitchell, a suite of plates of Holiday's drawings and related topics, and "The Listing of the Snark" by Selwyn Goodacre. It was issued in several formats:

a. Subscriber's edition—limited to 395 numbered copies, signed by the participants. Quarter leather, cloth board covers, with separate suite of the plates, all within publisher's box.

b. Collector's edition—limited to 1,995 copies. Red cloth boards, title, etc., on spine on black stick-on label.

c. Trade edition—5,000 copies. Black cloth boards, lettered in red, in red dust wrapper, Lettered in black and white with Holiday picture on the front. "Reprinted with emendations in February 1982."

d. The section "The Listing of the Snark" issued as a separate offprint of fifty-seven copies for Selwyn Goodacre.

1983 University of California Press, Berkeley. Illustrated by Barry Moser and with an Introduction by James R. Kincaid. Blue paper wrappers, with embossed title. Pp. 44. 34 × 21.3 cm. First trade edition. Also issued as:

a. Edition limited to one hundred copies numbered and signed by Moser, with five of the printed illustrations, signed by Moser, loosely inserted.

b. Published by the University of California Press for the Lewis Carroll Society of

North America as Carroll Studies Number 7 in a limited edition of 350, signed by Moser.

1989 Carroll Foundation, Flemington, Australia. Illustrated by Frank Hinder, with an introductory essay by John Paull and explanatory poems by Hinder. Black paperboards, with design and title, etc., on front cover and spine in gilt. Pp. 64. 24.6 × 19 cm. Also issued as a limited edition of one hundred copies signed and numbered by the illustrator, in white cloth boards.

1992 Lewis Carroll Society of North America, New York. Illustrated by Jonathan Dixon. First edition limited to 450 copies. Black cloth with pictures and title, etc., in silver. Also issued in a deluxe edition limited to fifty copies, each with an extra sketch. Bound as the standard edition but with pictures and title, etc., in gilt. A number of hand-colored prints from the book were also issued. Pp. 90. 27.9 × 21.2 cm.

1993 Macmillan, London. With an introduction by Selwyn Goodacre. The only edition to be printed, by the original publishers, from the original wood blocks. This was done by Ian Mortimer at his Press, I. M. Imprint, London. 25.9 × 18.2 cm. It was issued in several formats:

a. Numbers 1–55 bound in full leather and presented in a slipcase with a portfolio of separate prints of the nine wood-engravings;

b. Numbers 56–130 quarter bound in cloth over paperboards and presented in a slipcase with the prints;

c. Numbers 131–430 quarter bound in cloth over paperboards in a slipcase.

A trade edition was issued, without the Goodacre introduction. "A faithful photographic reproduction of the poem and its illustrations in the limited edition."

1994 Tome Press, Missouri. Illustrations by Henry Holiday. Paperback. Pp. 32. 25.6 × 92 cm.

1995 Privately printed by Gavin O'Keefe, Victoria, Australia. Illustrated by Gavin O'Keefe. Red paper wrappers, with paste-on white label with picture, title, etc., in black. Pp. 41. 21.1 × 14.7 cm.

1997 Angerona Press, Ryde, Isle of Wight. *The Hunting of the Snark Concluded*, by Cathy Bowern, illustrations by Brian Puttock. The book starts with the full text of the *Snark*, with Puttock illustrations. This is followed by Bowern's sequel, also illustrated by Puttock. Cream cloth boards, lettered on spine in gilt. Full-color dust wrapper. Pp. 121. 21 × 14.7 cm.

1997 Angerona Press, Ryde, Isle of Wight. *The Snark Decoded* by Cathy Bowern, illustrations by Brian Puttock. The full text of the *Snark*, and the sequel, are reprinted, now with full notes by Bowen on both. Paperback. Pp. 142. 21 × 14.7 cm.

2000 Privately printed, St. Petersburg. Text is hand written by Yuri Shtapakov and surrounded by hand-colored drypoint engravings. Quarto portfolio. Pp. 49. Housed in original folding case of multicolored leather onlays, with an inset featuring one of the engravings on each panel. A personal tour de force. Only two copies produced.

Translations

The countries are listed chronologically, in order of their first *Snark* translations.

FRENCH

1929 *La Chasse au Snark*, Hours Press (Nancy Cunard), Chapelle-Reanville-Eure. Translated by Louis Aragon, unillustrated. A limited edition of ten copies on Japon, numbered from 1 to 5, with five not for sale; and 350 copies on Alfa, numbered from 1 to 300, with fifty not for sale. Each copy signed by the translator. Red paperboards with title, etc., in both languages on the front cover in black. Pp. 38. 23 × 22 cm.

Reprinted by P. Seghers, Paris, in 1949. White wrappers, pp. 45, 18 × 11 cm, no illustrations. Reprinted again in 1962. Stiff wrappers, with a picture on the front cover in green and purple by Mario Prassinos, pp. 69, 16 × 13.3 cm. Also reprinted in 1959 in red cloth and in November 1980 as a paperback, with front cover picture by Patrick Vanhoutte.

1940 *La Chasse au Snark*, Librairie José Corti, Paris. Translated by Henri Parisot, unillustrated. A limited edition of 255 unnumbered copies, 5 on Madagascar and 250 on Alfa. Stiff white card wrappers, with title, etc., on the front cover in black. Pp. 32 (iii). 24.5 × 15.5 cm.

1945 *La Chasse au Snark, de suivide fantasmagorie et de Poeta Fit, Non Nascitur*, Seghers, Paris. Translated by Henri Parisot. Also includes "Fantasmagorie" and "Poeta Fit, Non Nascitur." White card wrappers, with title in red, the rest in black. Pp. 108, (iv). 19 × 14.3 cm. Edges uncut. Limited edition of sixty numbered copies on Fil Johannot, 2,000 on velin, some H.C.

1946 *La Chasse au Snark et Autres Poèmes*, Fontaine, Paris. Translated by Henri Parisot ("revue et corrigee"), illustrations by Gisele Prassinos. The additional poems are the two directly above, plus "Le Morse et le Charpentier, Assis sur une Barrière et Jabberwocky." White card wrappers, title, etc., in black, intertwining picture of the Snark (?) in green and red. Pp. 140 (plus one leaf) numbered from front cover. Limited edition of 7 numbered copies on vergé de Hollande, with "un dessin original de Gisele Prassinos," 25 on marais crèvecoeur, 1,500 on velin, plus some H.C.

1948 *La Chasse au Snark*, G.L.M., Paris. Translated by Florence Gilliam and Guy Levis Mano, illustrated by Henry Holiday. A limited edition of 1,080 copies, and 25 for "les amis de G.L.M." Includes the English text. There was a new edition in 1970, published by Le Club Français du Livre (pp. 146) and a further edition in 1980.

1950 *La Chasse au Snark*, **Editions** Premières, **Paris**. A new translation by Henri Parisot, illustrations by Max Ernst. In the series L'Age d'Or. Issued in a limited edition of 775 numbered copies, numbers 1–25 on marais crèvecoeur, with a signed and numbered color etching and an embossed design inscribed "Carte de l'océan" by Ernst, and numbers 26–775 on Alfama (there were a few copies "hors commerce"). Pp. 72. 16.7 × 13.2 cm.

1952 *Lewis Carroll, an Étude*, **P. Seghers, Paris**. A translation by Henri Parisot is included in his biography of Lewis Carroll (in the series Poètes d' Aujourd'hui). One of the Ernst illustrations is included.

1962 *La Chasse au Snark*, **Jean-Jacques Pauvert, France**. Translated by Henri Parisot, illustrations by Henry Holiday. A limited edition of 1,999 numbered copies, 1–30 on pur du marais, 31–1,999 on offset alfa bellegarde. Blue paper wrappers with the title, etc., in black on the front with a reproduction in the center of the first-edition cover—front and back on the front and back, in black and white. Pp. ix, 82. 18.2 × 13 cm.

1969 *Le Rire des Poètes*, **Pierre Belfond, Paris**. Translated by Henri Parisot. Pp. 26–76 are a selection of Carroll verses, including the *Snark*.

1971 *Through the Looking-Glass and The Hunting of the Snark*, Aubier-**Flammarion, Paris**. Translated by Henri Parisot, the *Snark* is on pp. 248–99. It is followed by a suite of illustrations by Max Ernst. The text in English is on the left-hand page, the French on the right. Stiff paper wrappers. The front cover has the title, etc., in brown and black, with a photograph of Dodgson below on the right, with a brown rectangle on the left. The back cover has the opening paragraph from *Looking-Glass* (bilingual) with the Dodgson photograph above. Pp. 318. 17.8 × 10.9 cm.

Reprinted in 1976, with an extended list of books at the end "dans la meme collection." Red stiff paper wrappers, with title, etc., in back and white and with a "butterfly blot" picture. On the back in white is "Lewis Carroll" and "en bilingue." The *Snark* is revised again.

In a letter to the present writer, M. Parisot stated that he first translated the *Snark* in 1940, and subsequently reworked it about ten times, before producing his definitive version for the Aubier-Flammarion bilingual edition in 1976.

1981 *La Chasse au Snark*, **Garance, Paris and Geneva**. Text français de Jacques Roubard, mise en image(s) de Annie-Claude Martin. Thirty-two separate sheets, printed on one side only; in printed red board case, with picture on the front cover. 32 × 25 cm.

1986 *Tout Alice et La Chasse au Snark*, **Editions Aubier Montaigne, France**. Translated by Henri Parisot, illustrated by Ralph Steadman.

1996 *La Chasse au Snark*, **Editions Mille et Une Nuits, France**. Translated by Bernard Hoepffner. Pp. 64. 15.5 × 10.5 cm.

1997 *La Chasse au Snark*, **Collection Théâtre d'Expressions, France**. Translated by Fabrice Eberhard, illustrated by Gregory Lhomme. Text in French and English. Paperback, pp. 114. 20 × 11.8 cm.

1998 *La Chasse au Snark*, **Bubble Gum News, France**. Translated by François Naudin. Card covers over loose sheets with spine binder. Pp. 20. 29.6 × 21.1 cm.

1999 *La Chasse au Snark*, **La Double vue La Différence, Paris**. Illustrated by Júlio Pomar, translated by Gerard Gacon, with essays by Gerard Gacon and Gerard-Georges Lemaire. Glazed paperboards with color pictures on front and back. Pp. 120. 23.7 × 29.5 cm.

LATIN

1934 *The Hunting of the Snark*, **Macmillan, London**. Rendered into Latin verse, in Virgilian hexameters, by Percival Robert Brinton, D.D. (Rector of Hambledon, Buckinghamshire). Unillustrated. English text is on the left-hand page, Latin on the right. Red paper wrappers, lettered in gilt, black blank. Pp. vi, 58. 19.3 × 13 cm.

1936 **The Hunting of the Snark, Shakespeare Head Press, sold by Basil Blackwell, Oxford**. Translated into Latin elegiacs by H. D. Watson, with a foreword by Gilbert

Murray. Unillustrated. English text is on the left-hand page, Latin on the right. Dark blue cloth boards, title, etc., on the front in gilt and on the spine. All edges uncut. The translation was directly inspired by the 1934 Brinton translation (above). The volume includes several other poems by the translator, along with their Latin translations. Pp. xvi, 116. 19 × 12.8 cm.

ITALIAN

1945 *La Caccia allo Snarco*, **Magi-Spinette, Rome**. Translated by Cesare Vico Lodovici. Illustrations by Ketty Castellucci. Pp. 79.

1985 *La caccia allo Squado*, **Studio Tesi, Italy**. Translated by Milli Griffi.

1989 *La Caccia allo Snark*, **S. E., Milan**. Translated and with an afterword by Roberto Sanesi. A bilingual edition, with the Holiday illustrations.

SWEDISH

1959 *Snarkjakten*, **Holger Schildts Forlag, Helsingfors**. Translated by Lars Forssell. Illustrations by Tove Jansson in line from pen-and-ink drawings. Stiff paper wrappers, the front cover off white with a picture in green, black, and blue; title, etc., in black, and also on the spine. The back cover has a drawing from the text. Pp. 56. 22 × 14.2 cm. Issued at 9.75 Kr.

DANISH

1963 *Snarkejagten*, Det Schonbergske Forlag, Copenhagen. Translated by Christopher Maaløe. English text on the left, Danish on the right. Paper wrappers; the front cover has a photographic reproduction of a fabric picture of a Snark with a bathing-machine sporting Union Jack wheels. Pp. 77. 22.3 × 15.7 cm.

GERMAN

1968 *Die Jagd nach dem Schnark*, Insel Verlag, Frankfurt am Main. Translated by Klaus Reichert. English text on the left-hand page, German on the right. Illustrations by Henry Holiday. Paperboards, the covers designed in the style of the first edition, but in purple on green, and with the addition of a paper label with the title, etc., and a similar label on the spine. The volume matches the edition of *Alice's Adventures in Wonderland* and *Letters to Child Friends*; all three volumes are in the series Insel-Bucherei. The *Snark* is "Nr. 934." Pp. 96. 18 × 11.6 cm.

New edition 1982, entirely reset, pale mauve paper wrappers. Front cover has the Bellman's uncle picture, with title, etc., all in black. Pp. 119. 17.6 × 10.7 cm.

1988 *Die Jagd nach dem Schnark*, Edition Weitbrecht, Stuttgart. An edition to accompany the musical version (see below). Includes the libretto, plus the full English text of the *Snark*. Pp. 143.

1996 *Die Jagd nach dem Schnark*, Philipp Reclam jun., Stuttgart. English and German edition. Translated by Oliver Sturm. Orange paper wrappers, with cover illustrations of the Banker's fate without the Bellman. Pp. 98. 14.8 × 9.7 cm.

SPANISH

1970 *La Caza del Snark*, Calatayud-Dea, Buenos Aires. Apparently a second edition. No details available of first publication, but the volume is illustrated. Pp. 75.

1971 *Le Caza del Snark*. Translated by Ulalume González de León. In *Plural*, no. 2, November 1971.

1980 *El Riesgo del Placer*, Biblioteca Era Poesia, Mexico. Includes *Le Caza del Snark*, translated by Ulalume González de León.

1982 *La Caza del Snark*, Ediciones Libertarias. Translated by Leopoldo Maria Panero, illustrated by Henry Holiday and Jesus Gaban.

1982 *La Caza del Snark*, Ediciones Mascaron. Translated by Maria Eugenia Frutos and J. J. Laborda, illustrated by Henry Holiday.

1986 *Alicia en el pais de las maravillas, Alicia a traves del espejo, La Caza del Snark*, Plaza y Janes Editores. Translated and with an introduction by Luis Maristany.

JAPANESE

1972 *Book of Modern Poetry Vol. 2: Lewis Carroll*, Shicho-sha, Yokyo. A translation by Junnosuke Sawazaki. The *Snark* is included on pp. 264–303.

1977 *Poems of Lewis Carroll*, Chikuma-shabou, Tokyo. Includes a translation of the *Snark* by Yasunari Takahashi and Junnosuke Sawazaki. Reprinted in a pocket-size edition in 1989.

Yoshiyuka Momma tells me of three Japanese books with *Snark* titles which in fact are not translations but are works inspired by the *Snark*.

POLISH

1973 Literatura na Świecie, no. 5. Includes a translation (*Wyprawa na Zxmireacza: Meka w Osmiu Konwujlsjach*) by Robert Stiller.

DUTCH

1977 *De Jacht op de Trek*, Uitgeverij J. Couvreur, The Hague. Translated by Erdwin Spits. Illustrations by Inge Vogel. Stiff paper wrappers in metallic green, with title, etc., and pictures in maroon. The front cover has the ship approaching with a large bird in the foreground; the back cover has the ship sailing away. Pp. 44. 19.3 × 3 cm.

1977 *De Jacht op de Strok*, Drukwerk, Amsterdam. Translated by Evert Geradts and with his own illustrations. Paperboards; the covers have a close design of green leaves on a yellow background, title in green in a white background; above is a circular paste-on picture of forks and "Hope" (represented as the upper half of a nude female figure); the back cover has a triangular paste-on picture,

again of "Hope," but with thimbles. Issued in a cellophane dust wrapper lettered in black, with author and translator, etc. The book ends with an eight-page "Nawoord" by Geradts, with a photograph. Pp. 104. 22.1 × 13.8 cm.

1987 *The Hunting of the Snark (A Delirium in Eight Crises)*, Dedalus, Antwerpen. Van Paul Pourveur naar Lewis Carroll: 1987. Paperback. Dramatized version. Accompanied by a 33-rpm LP record, with record sleeve and one sheet insert. All in a gray card box, decorated with Carroll's drawing of himself lecturing (with hand over mouth).

2001 *De Jacht op de Snark*, Hassink Drukkers, Haaksbergen. Translated and with annotations by Henri Riuzenaar, illustrated by Iris Cousijnsen. Blue paperboards, lettered in white, with full-color picture from the book. Back cover has a picture of Riuzenaar. Text includes English text. Limited to two hundred copies, in matching slipcase. 23 × 29 cm.

RUSSIAN

1982 *Ochota na Zmerya*. Translated by Vladimir Orel. In the Journal *Inostrannaya Literatura*, no. 10: 231–4.

1991 *Ochota na Snarka*, Rukitis, Moscow. Translated by Grigorii Krushkov, illustrated by Leonid Tishkov. Gray decorated paperboards. Pp. 88. 24 × 15.5 cm. There is a variant issue in white decorated paperboards.

1993 **Krug, Moscow.** Translated by I. Lipkin, illustrated by L Zaleskii. Blue paper wrappers.

1999 **Eksmo Press, Moscow.** Translated by Leonid Yachnin and Yuli Dumilov, introduction by Leonid Yachnin. Also includes the Alice books and *Letters to Children*. Pp. 606. 20 × 12.5 cm.

HEBREW

1989 **Shva Publishers, Israel.** Translated by Nitsa Ben-Ari, illustrated by Danny Kerman.

2000 **Israel.** Translated by Yony Lahav, illustrated by Ami Rubinger.

BULGARIAN

1993 **Xumono, Bapha.** Paperback. The *Snark* is on pp. 29–51. Also includes other nonsense verse and *A Tangled Tale*.

FAROESE

1994 *Eftir Snarki*, **Forlagio Sprotin.** Illustrated by Axel Torgard. Glazed card wrappers, with full-color picture on front cover, author and blurb on the back. English text included. Pp. 80. 24 × 17 cm.

Anthologies Including the Entire *Snark*

Although I hope most examples are included, I cannot claim that this section is comprehensive. Certain volumes which properly belong here have been listed or mentioned earlier: *Rhyme? And Reason?* because of its importance in the narrative of the early history; the Parisot French translations, for the sake of clarity and continuity; and a number because they present the *Snark* as the main feature of the book—1899 Burt, 1903 Newell, 1939 Chameleon, and the 1936 Watson Latin translation. For the sake of clarity, where translations occur in anthologies, they are included in the relevant translations section.

The books listed here are cited only in their first editions and are listed in chronological order.

Nonsense Anthology, collected by Carolyn Wells: Charles Scribner's Sons, New York, 1902. Includes "The Hunting of the Snark" (extract).

Alice's Adventures in Wonderland, Through the Looking-Glass and the Hunting of the Snark (introduction by Alexander Woollcott): Modern Library, Boni & Liveright, New York, 1924.

Alice in Wonderland, Through the Looking-Glass and Other Comic Pieces: Everyman's Library, Dent/Dutton, London/New York, 1929.

The Collected Verse of Lewis Carroll: E. P. Dutton & Co., New York, 1929.

Alice in Wonderland with The Hunting of the Snark and Poems from Sylvie and Bruno (ed. Guy N. Pocock): King's Treasuries of Literature, J. M. Dent, London, 1930.

The Lewis Carroll Book (ed. Richard Herrick): Dial Press, New York, 1931.

Alice's Adventures in Wonderland, Through the Looking-Glass and The Hunting of the Snark (introduction by Mrs. F. D. Roosevelt): Jacket Library, National House Library Foundation, Washington, D.C., 1932.

The Collected Verse of Lewis Carroll: Macmillan, London, 1932/The Macmillan Co., New York, 1933.

Logical Nonsense: The Works of Lewis Carroll (ed. Philip C. Blackburn and Lionel White): G. P. Putnam's Sons, New York, 1934.

Nonsensibus . . . , by. D. B. Wyndham Lewis: Methuen, London, 1936.

The Complete Works of Lewis Carroll (introduction by Alexander Woollcott): Random House, New York, 1936.

Poems Selected from the Works of Lewis Carroll: Macmillan, London, 1939.

Alice's Adventures in Wonderland, Through the Looking-Glass and The Hunting of the Snark: Carlton House, New York, undated but circa 1930s.

Alice's Adventures in Wonderland, Through the Looking-Glass and The Hunting of the Snark, with illustrations by John Tenniel: Blue Ribbon Books, New York, undated (1940s?).

Poets of the English Language, vol. 5, Tennyson to Yeats (ed. W. H. Auden and Norman Holmes Pearson): Viking Press, London, 1950.

The Humorous Verse of Lewis Carroll (ed. J. E. Morpurgo): Grey Walls Press, London, 1950. In the Crown Classics series.

Lewis Carroll's Alice in Wonderland and Other Favourites: Pocket Books, New York, 1951.

Alice's Adventures in Wonderland, Through the Looking-Glass and other Writings (introduction by Robin Deniston): Collins, London and Glasgow, 1954.

The Book of Nonsense by Many Authors (ed. Roger Lancelyn Green): Dent, London, 1956. In the Children's Illustrated Classics series.

The Silver Treasury of Light Verse (ed. Oscar Williams): New American Library, New York, 1957. A Mentor Book.

Lewis Carroll, Nonsense Verse: Edward Hulton, London, 1959. In the Pocket Poets series.

The Sapphire Treasury of Stories for Boys and Girls (ed. Gillian Avery): Gollanz, London, 1960.

The World of Victorian Humor (ed. Harold Orel): Appleton-Century-Crofts, New York, 1961.

Alice's Adventures in Wonderland, Through the Looking-Glass, and The Hunting of the Snark: Nonesuch Press, London, 1963 (published under the Bodley Head imprint in 1974). A Nonesuch Cygnet.

The Oxford Book of Nineteenth Century Verse (ed. John Hayward): Oxford University Press, London, 1964.

The Works of Lewis Carroll (ed. Roger Lancelyn Green): Spring Books, Paul Hamlyn, London, 1965.

Alice in Wonderland (ed. Donald J Gray): W. W. Norton, New York, 1971. A Norton Critical Edition.

Poems of Lewis Carroll, selected by Myra Cohn Livingston: Thomas Y. Crowell, New York, 1973.

The Illustrated Lewis Carroll (ed. Roy Gasson): Jupiter Books, London, 1978.

The Faber Book of Nonsense Verse (ed. Geoffrey Grigson): Faber, London, 1979.

The Complete Illustrated Works of Lewis Carroll (ed. E. Guiliano): Avenel Books, New York, 1982.

The Complete Illustrated Works of Lewis Carroll: Chancellor Press, London, 1982.

The Oxford Book of Narrative Verse (chosen and edited by Iona and Peter Opie): Oxford University Press, Oxford and New York, 1983.

The Complete Alice & The Hunting of the Snark, illustrated by Ralph Steadman: Jonathan Cape, London, 1986.

The Best of Lewis Carroll, illustrated by John Tenniel and Henry Holiday: Castle, New York, undated (circa 1992).

Utter Nonsense, illustrated by Henry Holiday and Harry Furniss: Folio Society, London, 1998.

The Complete Stories and Poems of Lewis Carroll: first published in 2001 by Geddes & Grosset, an imprint of Children's Leisure Products Limited, for Midpoint Press, New Lanark, Scotland, 2001.

Theatrical and Musical Adaptations, and Recordings

I am indebted to Charles Lovett's book *Alice on Stage* (Meckler, Westport, Conn., 1990) for details of many of the following productions.

1960 A reading by Boris Karloff: Caedmon Records. Includes "The Pied Piper."

1963 A reading by Alec Guinness on BBC radio on 24 December 1963. Alan Tannenbaum has a copy of the 34-page script.

Circa 1970 Adapted by Anthony Gash, presented at Magdalen College, Oxford University.

1971 Operatic version by Bill Tchakirides, presented by Systems Theater at the Whitney Museum, New York, September 1971.

1978 Operatic version presented by the Queens College Departments of Music and Drama and Theatre at the Queens College

Theatre, Queens, New York, 13–16 April 1978.

1980 A French version by Ludovic Flament was presented (no further details to hand).

1982 A French version by Jean-Marie Boyer, with music by Denis Lefebvre du Prey, was presented at the Théâtre Atelier du Luxembourg, Paris, as part of the Festival Foire Saint-Germain, 11 June–2 July 1982.

1982 Version presented by June Alleyn's School in London, 8–9 July 1982. An operetta with music specially written for the production with some traditional tunes added.

1982 *The Hunting of the Snark*, music by Douglas Young: Cameo Classics, Manchester, England. LP record.

1984. Version by R. E. Jackson, with music by David Ellis, presented by the Children's Musical Theatre of Mobile, Alabama, as a touring production.

Circa 1986 Portuguese production in Lisbon.

1987 Mike Batt's *The Hunting of the Snark* was first performed at the Royal Albert Hall in London on Wednesday, 1 April 1987. A subsequent full dramatization was produced on the London stage a year later and closed after only a few performances. An earlier LP record version was also issued.

1987 *Lewis Carroll's The Hunting of the Snark, a Musical Comedy*, by R. Eugene Jackson, music by David Ellis: I. E. Clark, Inc., Schulenburg, Texas. Gray paper wrappers, spine and lettering in orange.

1988 German version by Michael Ende, music by Wilfried Hiller, performed at the Staatstheater am Gartnerplatz, Munich, 16 January 1988.

1992 *Hunting of the Snark*, a musical interpretation by Anne Nordheim for trombone, organ, and electronic music: Euridice, Oslo. Recorded at a live concert in September 1991.

1993 *Alice in Wonderland*, CD-ROM: Queue, Inc., and Clearvue, Inc., Fairfield, Conn. Includes the *Snark*.

1999 Set of audio cassettes of works by Lewis Carroll, with extra notes. Includes the *Snark*. Entertainment Software, Inc., Commuter's Library, Ardington, Texas.

2000 Crazy Horse Theatre Company presented a dramatic version at the Museum of Oxo Tower Wharf, South Bank, London, 11–29 April 2000.

2002 *Jabberwocky, Stuff and Nonsense*, read by Griffin Rogers and Brianna Voss: Painted Wings Film, audio CD, with pictorial insert. Includes the *Snark*, read by Rogers.

Undated. French version presented at Théâtre de Plaisance, Paris.

Undated. Play based on the Alice books and the *Snark* at Belmont Elementary School (precise location unknown).

Candle-ends

1936 *A Rime of Three Worthies*, by Ashley Ohmsted: privately printed, Edgartown, Mass. A limited edition of ten numbered copies, composed at the office of the *Vineyard Gazette* and imprinted in the shop of the Martha's Vineyard Printing Co., Oak Bluffs, Mass. Green half-cloth, decorated paper-boards in green and beige on cream. This curiosity is a full-length parody of the *Snark*. It falls well short of the original. Pp. 22 plus four blank leaves at the beginning and three at the end. 23.9 × 15.5 cm.

1941 *The Snark Was a Boojum*, by Richard Shattuck: William Morrow, New York; Robert Hale, London. A mystery novel, each chapter beginning with four lines from the *Snark*.

1973 Complete manuscript of the *Snark*, transcribed and illustrated by Charles E. Wright. Unpublished—in the Edward Wakeling collection. Separate sheets, 35.3 × 27.8 cm. The transcription, in a fine personalized script, covers forty sheets, preceded by the title sheet, and a suite of fourteen sheets, each with one of the thirteen characters and the author. A fine production that one might think merits publication.

1975 The Caxton Club of Chicago issued a "keepsake" on the occasion of its meeting on 19 November 1975. Reproduces the map and three stanzas. Printed by David Woodward, designed by R. Hunter Middleton, and signed by both.

1976 *Fit for a Beaver: "Fit the First" from* THE HUNTING OF THE SNARK, by Lewis Carroll, illustrations by Byron Sewell, Chicken Little's Press, Austin, Texas. A limited edition of thirty numbered and signed copies. Tan paper wrappers with title and picture on the front cover in black matching the title page. One picture per verse, quite different from the Sewell full-length version (1974) noted above under English-Language Editions. Printed on side of the leaf only. Twenty-seven leaves. 28 × 21.5 cm.

1976 *The Hunting of the Snark, Fit the First*, by Lewis Carroll, illustrations by Byron W. Sewell, privately printed by Byron Sewell, Austin, Texas. A limited edition of eight numbered and signed copies. Black stiff card wrappers, with title, etc., on the front in gilt. The text, printed from the illustrator's own script, is on one side of the leaf only, apart from the title page, which has the imprint and copyright notice on the reverse. Each obverse merits a leaf to itself. The verses are interspersed at intervals with the illustrations which are hand-pulled lithographs in color on German etching paper. Each is mounted on gray card, protected by a tissue guard, and attached only at the top so that the title, limitation note, and signature in pencil can be read on the reverse. The pictures may be described as symbolic in style; the symbolism is more obscure in some than in others. Twenty-five leaves. 27.5 × 21.5 cm.

Byron Sewell continued to issue strange *Snark* items, many of them single sheets, in minute numbers in the years 2000 to 2004 (see below for his 2000 Millennium Snark Trilogy).

1983 *"Snark Island"* stamps. These are what are called, in the Philatelic world, "Cinderella stamps." Created by Gerald King. A priced catalogue, with an introduction by Selwyn Goodacre, was issued in May 1983.

1984 *The Hunting of the Snark—Fit the Ninth—the Homecoming*, written by Richard Garnett for the fiftieth anniversary of the Snark Club at King's College Cambridge, Wednesday, 30 May 1984. Fifty copies printed by Simon Rendall. Pp. 4 folded card. 19 × 12.8 cm.

1991 *The Hunting of the Snark*, a children's World War II play, by Bob Hescott and Stephen Cockett: Collins Educational, London.

1992 *The Cooking of the Snark Act II*: The Snarks Ltd., New York, 1992.

1996 *The Hunting of the Snark, Second Expedition*, by Peter Wesley-Smith, illustrations by Paul Stanish: Cherry Books, Camperdown, Australia.

1998 *The Hunting of the Snark, Eighth Fit*, translated into French without using the letter *e*, "traduire La Contrainte, Formules No. 2": L'Age D'Homme.

1998 *"The Booking"*—A Missing Fit from Lewis Carroll's *The Hunting of the Snark*, by Charlie Lovett: privately printed.

2000 *The Hunting of the Snark*, program for the Lewis Carroll Society Christmas Party, December 2000. Includes an essay on the *Snark* by Selwyn Goodacre. Six-page stapled booklet.

2000 *The Sorting of the Snark*, by Roger Scowen: TGB Productions, London. An alphabetical list of words in the *Snark*.

2000 *"The Recrewting"* and *"The Sailing,"* two unpublished fits from Lewis Carroll's sequel to *The Hunting of the Snark*, by Charlie Lovett: privately printed.

2000 *Atchafalaya Boojum*, by Byron W. Sewell: Thousand Oaks Press, Calgary, 2000. An edition of ten copies, signed by the author.

2000 *Snark! A Murderous Agony in Eight Fits*, by Byron Sewell: Thousand Oaks Press, Calgary, 2000. An edition of ten copies, signed by the author.

2000 *Snarkmaster*, by Byron Sewell: Storkling Press, Dead Deer, Alberta, Canada. An edition of fifteen copies, signed by the author. (These last three items, Sewell informs me, are what he calls his Millennium Snark Trilogy).

2002 *Alice & The Snark*, by Everett Bleiler: Snark's Cave, New York, 2002. A limited edition of thirty-five numbered copies. A book of essays mainly about the *Snark*. Pp. 80. 20.5 × 14.8 cm.

2003 *The Translating of the Snark*, by Selwyn Goodacre and Mark R. Richards: Aznet Publishing, London. An attempt to list all known translations of the *Snark*.

2004 *A Snark Selection*, illustrated by Gavin O'Keefe, with Snarkian chapters by Harry Stephen Keeler: Ramble House, Shreveport, La.

2005 *Square Snark*, words by Lewis Carroll, edited by Alan Tannenbaum: privately printed. The *Snark* "translated" into Lewis Carroll's nyctograph script.

HUNTING THE *SNARK*
ON THE WEB

Much of the web-based information related to Lewis Carroll's *The Hunting of the Snark* falls into two areas. There are websites chronicling Carroll's entire works, and sites that focus almost entirely on the poem. Strangely, these two domains seem to be separated from one another. If your focus is almost exclusively on the *Snark*, start with Wikipedia's *Hunting of the Snark*. You will not find much information about the *Snark* on the Lewis Carroll websites, but you will find plenty of information on the author. Happy hunting!

Lewis Carroll

The Lewis Carroll Society. This appears to be the most comprehensive website exhibiting conventional literary and historical information on the life and work of Lewis Carroll. http://lewiscarrollsociety.org.uk/

Lewis Carroll Society of North America. This is where you will find information about North American events examining/discussing the work of Lewis Carroll. www.lewiscarroll.org/

Lewis Carroll Home Page. This site is a combination of conventional information and less conventional (e.g., logic, math, and games) and pop-culture-related links. www.lewiscarroll.org/carroll.html

The Lewis Carroll Scrapbook Collection. The Library of Congress's digitization (e.g., ability to view individual pages) of a scrapbook that contains material Carroll collected between the years 1855 and 1872. According to the site's introduction, there are approximately 130 digitized items, representing a collection of newspaper clippings, photographs, and manuscript materials. http://international.loc.gov/intldl/carrollhtml/lchome.html

References

Wikipedia's *The Hunting of the Snark*. The most structured and comprehensive website in terms of presenting the *Snark*'s characters, content, plot, and impact on literature and society.

http://en.wikipedia.org/wiki/The_Hunting_
of_the_Snark

Poetry Archive's Lewis Carroll Section. A collection of more than twenty-five of Carroll's poems, including *The Hunting of the Snark*, "Jabberwocky," and "The Walrus and the Carpenter." www.emule.com/poetry/?page=overview&author=34

Online Versions of
The Hunting of the Snark

Each of the links below will take you to an online version of *The Hunting of the Snark*. Some are text-only versions, whereas others include some or all of Henry Holiday's illustrations. Each provides a unique representation of the poem.

www.literature.org/authors/carroll-lewis/the-hunting-of-the-snark/

http://naiades.com/Snark/

www.gutenberg.org/etext/13

www.pacificnet.net/~johnr/books/books.html

www.theotherpages.org/poems/carrol103.html

http://etext.library.adelaide.edu.au/c/carroll/lewis/snark/index.html

www.readprint.com/work-178/Lewis-Carroll

www.unm/edu/~keith/theHuntingOfTheSnark.html

Henry Holiday (Illustrator)

Henry Holiday. This site is the most comprehensive listing of information on Henry Holiday, who illustrated the *Snark*. As you will discover, Holiday was not primarily an illustrator of books. He is best known as a designer of stained-glass church windows. www.visitcumbria.com/holiday.htm

Holiday's *Dante and Beatrice* Painting. This is Holiday's most well known painting. www.liverpoolmuseums.org.uk/picture-of-month/displaypicture.asp?venue=2&id=152

Various Others

"Snark"—*Stanford Encyclopedia of Philosophy*. A whimsical definition of Snarks, addressing characteristics of their contemporary (e.g., post twentieth century) habitat and adaptive features. http://plato.stanford.edu/entries/sample/

Equator—*The Hunting of the Snark*. An interactive problem-solving game for children, based on the poem, which includes the use of technology tools. www.informatics.sussex.ac.uk/interact/projects/Equator/snark.htm

The Snark Club of Cambridge University. A club with the sole purpose of glorifying *The Hunting of the Snark*. Note its highly unambiguous rules. www.wizardwheeze.com/snark/

ABOUT THE EDITOR

Martin Gardner is the author or editor of more than 100 books and booklets, including books on mathematics, science, pseudoscience, philosophy, literary criticism, and fiction (including *Visitors from Oz*, based on L. Frank Baum's *The Wonderful Wizard of Oz*). Gardner is also the annotator of a number of classic literary works from *The Night Before Christmas* and Gilbert K. Chesterton's *The Innocence of Father Brown* to Coleridge's *The Ancient Mariner*. Gardner's annotated version of *Alice in Wonderland*, *The Annotated Alice*, has sold more than 50,000 copies worldwide. At ninety-one, Martin Gardner has influenced and inspired generations of scientists, scholars, and nonscientists. Stephen Jay Gould once said that Martin Gardner "has become a priceless national resource," a writer "who can combine wit, penetrating analysis, sharp prose, and sweet reason into an expansive view that expunges nonsense without stifling innovation, and that presents the excitement and humanity of science in a positive way."

ABOUT ADAM GOPNIK

Adam Gopnik has been writing for *The New Yorker* for more than twenty years, where he has served as art critic and Paris correspondent, and he now writes, among other things, its New York Journal. His first book, *Paris to the Moon*, a collection of essays about his five years in France, became a national bestseller, and has been called "the finest book on France in recent years." He is also the author of *The King in the Window*, an adventure story, and of the forthcoming *Through the Children's Gate*, a collection of essays about the past five years in New York. He has won the National Magazine Award for Essays and for Criticism three times, as well as the George Polk Award for magazine reporting.